LOVE UNDER FIRE

by Valden Bush

2025

BUTTERWORTH BOOKS

Butterworth Books is a different breed of publishing house. It's a home for Indies, for independent authors who take great pride in their work and produce top quality books for readers who deserve the best. Professional editing, professional cover design, professional proof reading, professional book production—you get the idea. As Individual as the Indie authors we're proud to work with, we're Butterworths and we're *different*.

Authors currently publishing with us:

E.V. Bancroft
Valden Bush
Addison M Conley
Jo Fletcher (JL Fletcher)
Helena Harte
Lee Haven
Karen Klyne
Sydney Lear
AJ Mason
Ally McGuire
James Merrick
Robyn Nyx (RJ Nyx)
JP Preston
Simon Smalley
JJ Thomas
Brey Willows

For more information visit www.butterworthbooks.co.uk

This trade paperback is published by Butterworth Books, UK

CATALOGING INFORMATION
ISBN: 978-1-915009-95-1
CREDITS
Editors: Victoria Villaseñor & Nicci Robinson
Cover Design: Nicci Robinson
Production Design: Global Wordsmiths

Acknowledgements

I'm so pleased that you've enjoyed my books. I write them because I have stories bubbling in my head, and they were the sort of books I wanted to read when I was younger and could never find. Knowing I'm bringing you pleasure makes my writing worthwhile

Despite having written a plethora of short stories and this being my fourth book, I feel as if I'm still a babe in my writer journey. They say it takes a village to produce a child, and in my world, the word child should be replaced by book. I'm still learning; and that includes re-learning as I make mistakes and forget what I already know!

My village has a few people I need to thank. Without them, this book wouldn't have happened. Firstly, Nicci Robinson and Victoria Villaseñor have once again allowed me to produce something I can be proud of, having continued to provide the knowledge and support that I've needed. They've been patient, as always, with my tardiness, bloops, and forgetfulness. They've encouraged me when I've doubted myself, and I know I couldn't have done this without them. Thank you.

Secondly, Gill Author (so named because I have a number of friends called Gill and have to differentiate them: Gill Brunch and

Gill Navy are the other two!). Gill is my author wife and continues to provide a safe space for us to discuss our stories, plotlines, doubts, and life in general. Thank you for always being there and for the laughs and joy you give.

Finally, thanks must go to my wife. Thank you seems too small a thing to say for the time she spends listening to my woes around plot holes and dialogue errors, and before she suggests their replacements. She spends a lot of time responding to things like, "What's another word for bullet?" as I explain I've already used it in the sentence before. She still gives me lots of cuddles and keeps me fed with all those vegetables she's grown. I love you.

Dedication

To G, my forever love.

CHAPTER ONE

ALEX HARTLEY LEANED BACK in her deckchair and closed her eyes, breathing in the salty sea air and luxuriating in the warm summer sunshine as it brushed across her skin. This was the kind of life she'd been working toward for years, and now she could enjoy it.

"You're not so old that you need an afternoon nap, are you?"

Alex's eyes sprang open at the interruption, and she looked up just in time to get a face full of ice-cold water from her friend, Flick.

"Argh!" Alex grabbed a towel and dried her face. "All done with your mother's birthday party then?"

"Yep." Flick held her wife's hand and guided her into a chair opposite Alex before flopping into her own.

Alex smiled at the gesture. Flick and Zamira seemed so perfectly matched, and boy, did she want what they had. Occasional one-night stands and short-term relationships had yet to find her the soulmate she craved. "It's good to see you both. How's life in Paris? Bad enough that you're going to move back here, I hope."

"The flat we were thinking about renting fell through," Flick said. "My uncle is happy for us stay in his place, but we want something we can put our own stamp on. We're thinking of buying somewhere outside Paris and just staying in the city when we need to. The trouble is we both love it so much, and it's difficult to leave the kind of life we have."

Zamira smiled. "It is very good to have café au lait and croissants on Saturday mornings, watching the world go by in one of our favorite squares. We have the tea, too, later in the day after walking along the Seine. C'est très romantique."

"I'm sure it is. Single women like me do similar things in London but somehow, it doesn't feel the same," Alex said.

"Yeah, but there are plenty of single women in Paris. They come out with their dogs and their newspapers or their embroideries, and they sit in the same cafes, enjoying the romance in the air." Flick tilted her glass toward Alex. "It's all about a state of mind, and we need to get you into it."

"Ha! Can you imagine me sitting knitting at a café in Covent Garden? No, no, no." Alex laughed. "I'd get random people sitting at my table giving their advice on stitches and offering to swap patterns."

Flick raised her eyebrow. "And how *is* your love life?"

"What love life?" Alex asked. "There's no love in my life. The end."

"You must have friends," Flick said. "What about Clare and Davina? Are they still around?"

Alex sighed. "Yes, but it's different now I'm their boss. They're still holding court and organizing events, which include everyone. But it's the same people every time, and I need to meet *new* people. I've tried going to a couple of the gay bars on my own, and all I end up doing is spending the night with someone I never want to see again. What is it about the average lesbian in London? I just don't want to spend any time with them."

"Maybe you've had sex with all the unattached ones, and the ones that are left don't do it for you?" Flick grinned.

"Don't be rude. I may have slept with a few women in my search." It might've been more than a few, but she wasn't about to admit that to Flick. "Maybe you're right. I wish I had your magnetism; you meet a woman, and she sticks to you like glue," Alex said.

"Yeah," Flick's gaze dropped, and she sighed deeply, "but it can be hard when you lose them."

Zamira moved onto Flick's lap and put her arms around her, glancing at Alex with a raised eyebrow.

"Oh god, Flick. I'm sorry. I wasn't thinking." Alex slapped her forehead. "I was just talking about Zamira." How insensitive could she be? It'd been two years since the death of Flick's first wife, but it was clear the grief was still raw.

Flick rubbed Zamira's arm. "It's okay. I know what you meant. Sometimes I still get overwhelmed, and words draw me back to places I don't want to go to. Luckily, Zamira can get me out of it one way or another."

Alex nodded, and an awkward silence ensued. "So how do I spice up my life? Before you got here, I was thinking about how I've got all the things I wanted: my own place, a well-paid job, and a sea view. I thought I'd be content. But no. I want someone to share it with." She looked out toward the sea, unseeing. "Please stop me from saying anything more embarrassing." The loneliness that had swept through her last night was so deep, it took her breath away. *But why now?*

"You'll have to volunteer for a job like I did. You pushed me to take that mission to Tarinor, saying it was just the thing I needed to do." Flick winked at Zamira. "And I ended up with the love of my life. I'll call Mary and tell her to find you a project."

Alex shook her head. "But I haven't done many front-line jobs. I'm all about diplomacy and high-level strategy."

"Yes, and you're damn good at it, which is why they promoted you to run the office. They didn't need my blunt-say-what-I-think viewpoint. Let's face it, you did nearly all my liaising when I was in that seat."

"Yeah, and I know I'm good at it. But nothing has come up for me in Africa recently. I suppose it's like with you and Tarinor. Nothing happens that needs your skills for a couple of years, and then there's a job with your name all over it."

"I'd forgotten that you came from the Special Intelligence Service in Africa," Flick said.

That wasn't surprising. Alex didn't talk a lot about her past; she'd rather talk about the things in front of her. "I was undercover mostly, but I was usually playing a lowly minion in some office or embassy, which gave me freedom to run things the way I wanted to. The easiest way to hide is to be in plain sight." She remembered when she'd been young and invincible, and every day was exciting, when the bad days were distant memories.

"Zamira, you should have seen her." Flick nudged her wife. "Using her guise of a ditzy white woman with little common sense, she was able to infiltrate places to get intelligence from people who underestimated her knowledge of the people, the language, and the country."

"It is hard to think of you as the fool," Zamira said. "You must be a good actress. You are so clever, even without a university degree to say so."

Alex kept her expression neutral, though the last part stung just a little.

"Believe me," Flick said, "she was extremely successful, and people in the SAS and SIS still talk about her work out there. You need to ask my brother Pete when we get home. He's got some stories—"

"Oh, no, Pete will tell you more than you need to know." Alex laughed, and heat rose up her neck. "There were one or two liaisons that he knows about. In most of those countries, lesbian and gay relationships are illegal, and anyone found guilty can expect the death penalty, so I was nun-like. It was when I got home that I had fun." She leaned back in her deckchair. "I don't need to be the ditzy woman anymore. I have a lot of useful skills, which is why I came to Department 6. I started off working out of Central Africa, helping to secure the release of mistreated women and imprisoned lesbians." Alex shrugged. "But since I transferred, it's been almost entirely paperwork and phone calls."

"I need a beer." Flick got up and pulled a few bottles from the cooler. She handed them to Alex and Zamira before dropping back into her seat. "What you need is an incredibly hot woman who makes you want to spend as little time at the office or on the road as possible."

"What I need is a diplomatic incident in Africa that uses my knowledge and language skills of Minabo, Delanda, and Rethan." Sure, the possibility of a woman to come home to was a nice one, but a new project was far more likely than a love interest.

"Be careful what you wish for." Flick wrapped her arms around Zamira and shivered. "I could do with some warmer weather. I'd forgotten how cold this coast can be. I need another sweater."

"I'll get you both one." Alex stood. "Let's go sit in the sunroom and forget that there's nothing between us and the North Pole but ice and water." Which wasn't so different from their conversation. Light and dark were relative, like cold and warm. Without shelter, bitter winds were colder, and time wiped away memories like mist from a windscreen. She shook away the thought and focused on her friends. Life could be short in this business, and not being present was a waste of something precious.

The following afternoon, Alex took Flick and Zamira to Heathrow. She dropped them off outside departures and struggled to keep her emotions in check. Her eyes watered, and she had a sinking feeling in her stomach.

Flick gave her a big hug. "Be patient. You've worked hard to get where you are, and something will come along when you least expect it. We love you."

Zamira joined the hug. "Talk to us soon with the news of your new project."

Alex was sad to leave them, but they'd given her a little seed of hope that things could change. As she pulled into traffic, the sound of horns blaring and tempers fraying receded into white noise. There were things she couldn't control but right now, she didn't have to stay put. She'd head home and then figure out the rest of the day.

After a typically hellish drive back to her apartment, she looked around. The furniture was all from secondhand shops and most of it didn't match. The bedroom, visible beyond the living room-kitchen-diner, had the only new piece of furniture, which was her bed. Her own minuscule piece of London, which allowed her to afford her true home in Norfolk, was little more than a shoebox with detritus she could sit on. She picked up her wallet, slipped on her wool jacket, and headed out. If she stayed here any longer, she'd get too maudlin, overthinking everything. She needed company, and she knew exactly where she could find some.

CHAPTER TWO

YESTERDAY, MITCH BRENNAN HAD been in Texas. Or was it the day before? Her internal clock was skewed, and jetlag made her stomach churn at the smell of burned coffee as she passed an airport café. She and her colleague, H, had been pulled off their project to come to London with the boss for a conference, and she had no idea how he thought they could help. Her reputation for being over-enthusiastic, gung-ho, and making quick decisions was stalling and fucking up her promotion chances. Maybe the colonel was looking at making her a paper-pusher in an office. She snorted out loud. Good luck with that. She was a doer. She always had been and wasn't going to start overthinking her way through life. That way only led to ruin.

The cab ride to the Excelsior Hotel was smooth enough to let her take a nap, and she wiped away a bit of drool when it stopped. A quick glance told her this building was no different from the others on the street. Old, heavy, pretentious. She kept her thoughts to herself as they registered at the reception. She walked to her room through the museum-like building full of old paintings, and H giggled like a kid at the stuffy silence. After dumping their luggage, they were ushered to a room. It had a vaulted ceiling, a couple of murals, chandeliers, and a huge screen at the front. She flopped into her seat with a sigh. What she wouldn't give for a bed right now.

"Good morning, and welcome to the US and UK co-international conference on crime and security across borders. Thank you to those of you who have traveled from the US for this important sharing of information. We'll go straight into our welcome talk from the US ambassador to the UK, Jessica Landen," the suit with the gray hair said.

Ms. Landen was a small, good-looking woman wearing clothes Mitch probably couldn't afford even with a pay raise. She sighed loudly, and H nudged her.

"We've traveled miles to get here, and we've got five days off work, so let's enjoy ourselves. You sitting here sighing is going to drive me nuts. So, we'll take in the sessions that might be interesting and the rest, we ignore. Okay?"

"Okay. I'll sit quietly through the rah-rah speech, and we can decide what to do over coffee." Mitch closed her eyes as Ms. Landen began to speak. Her spiel was no different from a dozen other speeches Mitch had heard, and within five minutes, she'd zoned out completely. She looked out of the window at the gray London sky and saw the murky River Thames outside the windows. Where would she go to meet some women? She and H would split up when she went in search of female company, and H wouldn't stir far from the hotel bar while she searched for her evening's entertainment.

She blinked, startled awake by half-hearted applause as the first session ended. They left the conference hall and headed for the foyer that was serving coffee, tea, and cookies, although the English called them biscuits, and they were dry, crumbly things more likely meant for farm animals. They were grabbed by Colonel Mike "Paddy" Ryan, their boss. "Come on, ladies, I want you to meet the ambassador."

Mitch rolled her eyes, but she and H followed Paddy like lambs to the slaughter.

"Ambassador, I'd like to introduce Sergeant Henrietta Richards, and Lieutenant Mitch Brennan who've come over from Texas. They're seconded from Homeland Security to the Bureau of Immigration and Customs Enforcement. They're often undercover with ICE, but I've pulled them into the daylight so that they can see the problems we face are worldwide and not just in the US."

Ms. Landen shook Mitch's hand. It was cool and limp, and up close, Mitch could see her perfect makeup and the gold necklace and bracelet she wore, likely worth more than a year's salary. This wasn't her world and based on the trappings of wealth or show, would never be.

"Thank you for traveling so far," Ms. Landen said. "I hope you get something from your visit."

"Yes, ma'am. I'm sure it will be useful—"

Before she could say anything more, the ambassador had turned away.

"If I wasn't already so cynical, I could be offended," Mitch said and laughed. She could see Paddy Ryan in the distance, chatting with a couple of British marine colonels. "Come on, we've been let loose. Let's find out when the seminars about people-smuggling are being held, so we can plan our day."

After a late lunch and two surprisingly useful sessions discussing links between smuggling groups, Mitch headed for her room. There was nothing she wanted to do for the rest of the day that would beat a nap to combat the jetlag. She dropped onto her bed, still in her jeans and sweater, her body weary and her mind overloaded. Irritated when sleep didn't come right away, she forced herself into the shower. The seminar discussions had taken her back to her last op, when she led a team undercover over the border into Mexico. They were still trying to tie down one of the smuggling rings, and her black ops team had been working for six months on a couple of leads. They'd watched an address in the hills where the gang had been collecting people to take over the border, but there hadn't been any movement, and it had grown tedious, with everyone on edge. Mitch didn't like it, but despite her feeling that something was wrong, she had to let the scenario play out the way the bosses had told her to. It was totally unlike her, but she did what was expected: she sat and waited. When they finally went in, the hacienda was almost deserted except for some family retainers. They eventually found a container truck abandoned behind thick foliage. Mitch had seen a lot of harrowing shit in her career, but the smell of that container and what was in it was something that she'd never forget. Whenever she closed her eyes, she saw the people left to die in what had become a tin can during a heatwave. She managed to lose the vision after a few days but whenever she was tired, it came back...along with the smell.

She would never hesitate again.

She wiped away steam from the mirror and noticed the dark circles under her eyes. They didn't matter. No one here would care, and she needed people to take her mind off the past as well as the mind-numbing present. Looking through her phone, she saw that a lesbian bar close by was already open. A few drinks and some female company were just what the doctor ordered.

Mitch took the short walk, needing the exercise and fresh air to clear her mind. Back in Texas, she had some favorite bars where she and her team partied hard. There were men and women from uniform professions who hung out together, and with them, she felt understood. A firefighter or a medic, it didn't matter. All of them put themselves on the line to keep the peace, to keep evil from taking over. A disease, a bad fire, or an explosion—that was where they ended their day. The sights and sounds that were part of their lives were something most of them re-lived in quiet moments. Some of her team had wives and partners that they ran to when they were overwhelmed, but like a lot of the single people, she drank, drank some more, and then found a beautiful woman to help her fall deeper into oblivion.

The bar was the only lesbian place in London and would give her that kind of peace, though it probably wouldn't be filled with people in uniform. As long as it served alcohol and she could find a warm body to take away the chill of her thoughts, she'd be happy.

She found the bar down an unassuming street and was surprised to find the entrance guarded by a female security guard. An almost hidden, underground bar was a sad state of affairs in London, which was supposed to be the ultimate in cosmopolitan cities. But the door at the bottom opened into a large, well-lit seating area with a dance floor at the far end. It wasn't busy yet, but she could see women in business suits, as well as a number in casual gear. *Home, sweet home.* She ordered herself a beer from a red-haired bartender and sat with her back to the bar looking around. Maybe not a wealth of options, but a few were possibilities.

"Are you visiting London? I haven't seen you in here before," a voice said from behind her.

She turned to the bartender. Her long hair curled at the ends, and her bangs framed her angular face. She looked at Mitch like she was starving, and Mitch was a double cheeseburger. "I s'pose you've never used that line before?" Mitch laughed. "But to answer your question: yeah, I'm visiting, and no, I haven't been here before. I'm in the city for a few days on business and thought I'd taste the night life."

"Shame I'm working. I would have enjoyed showing you the sights," the bartender said. "If you haven't found someone to give you a tour by the end of the evening, let me know and I'll give you a late-night excursion."

There was no mistaking what that might entail, given the gleam in her eyes. "Thank you. I'm Mitch, by the way," she said.

"Sparrow." Her hand lingered in Mitch's, and she gave a practiced, knowing smile.

After that, Sparrow was called away to serve other customers, and Mitch resumed her hunt. She moved to a table at the side of the bar, next to a group of women obviously having an after-work party. There could be someone there who'd want some company and would break away from the group. They seemed to be calling for more rounds though, leading Mitch to rethink. They were going to be too drunk to stand, let alone entertain a stranger. She finished her beer and went back to the bar, where there was a different bartender. Mitch ordered beer and a burger and sat at a table on the other side of the room. It didn't take her long to figure out she was sitting beside a woman at the next table who was also scoping out the room. *Potential.* "The partygoers were a little rowdy. I didn't want my burger to get a beer wash, so I moved."

"I don't blame you," the stranger said. "But give them half an hour, and they'll be gone."

"How can you tell?" Mitch asked.

"It's after-work drinks, and they'll be on trains to suburbia before eight p.m.—*if* they ever find the station or their train." She shook her head and gave Mitch a quick smile. "Sometimes you just know, you know?"

Mitch nodded and was about to respond when another group of women came in and joined the stranger. *Damn.* She was striking out all over the place. She should just eat and go get some sleep.

One of the new arrivals, a dark-haired woman with an undercut, turned to Mitch. "I saw you talking to Alex a moment ago," she said. "Would you like to join us?"

"That'd be great. I'm Mitch." She turned her chair around and moved the table out of the way.

"I'm Clare, that's Alex, and on the other side of her is Davina. And that over there is Magda. We tend to meet here a couple of evenings a week, to dance or watch the show. There are others, but they're on holiday."

Mitch's burger arrived before she needed to act interested in that random information, and she ordered a double Jack to wash it down. Then she ate, letting the conversation flow around her. The music had gotten louder, but she could still hear the chat.

"Is the food okay?" Alex asked.

"Yeah, not bad for England," she said and smiled.

"Okay, so you're from the US of A. One of those big beef-eating states, I suppose."

Her blue eyes looked Mitch over as she smiled, and her gaze made Mitch's skin tingle. She imagined Alex's hands moving over her body. She was so ready for that. Alex smiled knowingly.

"If you call Texas a big beef-eating state, you'd be right. Just got in," Mitch said. She wasn't one to give much information about herself. Her clandestine world encouraged obfuscation; lies and truth were often indistinguishable, just as they needed to be. Texas was a truth, and that was more than she usually gave anyone.

The rest of the group talked as best they could over music that had now reached a crescendo. Mitch needed to dull the edge a little more. She'd get laid, or she'd go back to her hotel and sleep well. Either would work at this point. She turned to Alex. "I'm getting myself a large bourbon. Do you want anything?"

"Scotch would be good, thanks," Alex said.

"You've met Clare and her crowd," Sparrow said when Mitch got the bar. "They'll be good company for a chat, if nothing else. If you're still feeling lonely, don't forget me when I get off at midnight."

"I'm hoping to be gone earlier, but thanks for the offer. I'm here for a few days, so maybe I can take you up on that another night." Mitch took the drinks back to the table. She drank hers quickly, and Alex matched her sip for sip until their glasses were empty.

"I'll return the favor," Alex said.

Mitch watched her walk away, her hips swaying in time to the music, her small waist just begging to be grasped and held. She laughed at something one of the other women said but didn't take her eyes from Alex, who moved sensually to the rhythm while waiting for Sparrow to pour their drinks. When she turned and made her way back, she held Mitch's gaze, setting her on fire.

"Dance?" Mitch asked, already half-standing. She held out her hand, and Alex set the drinks down and took a step back toward the dance floor.

Holey Moley, she was tall. Maybe three or four inches taller than Mitch. And God, was she beautiful. Her long legs led to her lovely ass, which Mitch couldn't take her eyes off as she followed Alex onto the dance floor.

The dance floor wasn't crowded, and they had plenty of space to move. Mitch let the music flow through her. They came together, still moving fast but somehow in perfect sync. Alex moved away and continued dancing before coming closer again, a perfect push-pull that set Mitch on fire. This was exactly what she'd come looking for: a woman who knew how to use her body, someone to drown out the world with her passion, someone to take away her pain.

As the music finished, and the DJ announced a short break, Mitch pulled Alex close. "I'm staying at the Excelsior. Would you like an early nightcap?"

"Mm." Alex pressed her body closer to Mitch.

The heat was intense, and Mitch wondered how she'd survive until she could get this woman into her bed. It was a long time since she'd been so turned on just from dancing. The way Alex moved had her entranced, as if she had magic coming out of her body. She held open Alex's jacket for her, waved at the group of friends who simply laughed, and walked out into the damp, chilled night air. Mitch wasn't sure what to say, but Alex made words unnecessary. She pushed Mitch into a narrow alleyway and kissed her hard, her slim body pressed the length of Mitch's. When they broke apart, Mitch took her hand and set off toward her hotel with nothing on her mind but Alex's skin under her hands.

In the hotel elevator, Alex pressed against her before the doors closed. Her makeup was perfect and highlighted her eyes and high cheekbones, and Mitch couldn't wait to see the rest of her. The ping of the elevator forced them apart, and she led Alex down the corridor to her room.

She was a master of this moment. Normally, she'd get her conquest's clothes off quickly, followed by her own, and they'd be on the bed in the blink of an eye. But tonight, for some reason, she didn't want to rush. She kissed Alex's neck gently before moving up to her mouth. Alex held her tightly, and Mitch leaned into her. She slipped her hands down Alex's back until she had her ass in her hands, and then she broke away.

Mitch tugged at her own shirt. "Do you want to join me or watch me?"

"Watch." Alex smirked and adjusted the lighting before she sat in the armchair by the window.

Mitch slowly unbuttoned her shirt, then she removed it and her tank top that was under it. The distance between her and Alex was too much, though. She could handle being exposed but stripping for someone wasn't as easy as the club girls made it look.

She moved to the armchair, straddled Alex and kissed her, long and slow. Then she stood and removed her jeans and socks, leaving her in her boxer shorts and her thin sports bra, her nipples pressing almost painfully against the material. She removed it and grinned at Alex's wide-eyed stare. She took her breasts in her hands and rubbed them gently, and Alex bit her bottom lip.

Mitch removed her boxer shorts and returned to straddle Alex's lap. As she got into place, Alex pulled Mitch toward her. Mitch could've exploded at the way Alex took charge so naturally, and she wanted to be open to anything Alex did to her, though that wasn't the way she usually operated. Alex put her hand between Mitch's legs and ran her fingers along her length. Mitch took a deep breath and inhaled the air that smelled of Alex's perfume and her own need for sex.

Alex entered her, thrusting in a steady rhythm. Mitch's need spiraled, and she was lost in the moment and the feelings before she came in an explosion that left stars behind her eyelids as she threw her head back and cried out.

Once she could draw breath, Mitch leaned back on her haunches. She became conscious of the fact that she was kneeling naked over Alex, who grinned. She got up and dropped back onto the bed. "I need to see you naked now. It's time for my show."

Alex removed her clothing slowly and carefully laid it out flat on the chair. Mitch could hear her breathing and figured that this pace was pushing the limits of her control. *Good to know it isn't just me.* Eventually, Alex stood before her in just a lacy red bra and matching bikini panties, with her hands on her hips and her expression expectant.

"Let me help you with that." Mitch slid across the bed and

unhooked Alex's bra, then let it slide down her arms until it dropped to the floor. She took Alex's nipple into her mouth and sucked gently. Alex grasped Mitch's head and moaned softly, her fingers tight in Mitch's hair. Mitch shifted to her other breast and slowly pushed Alex's panties down. Then she pulled Alex onto the bed, never breaking contact with her nipple.

She loved this part. Complete closeness, body to body, skin to skin. She lay down on top of Alex and reveled in the fleeting intimacy. It wouldn't last, but for the moment, it was divine.

Mitch kissed Alex gently before moving her hand down her stomach to explore the wetness below. Alex shuddered as she ran her fingers between her thighs. She concentrated on spots that made Alex's cries just a little louder. Finally, Alex's hips rose from the bed.

"Please," she said.

Mitch entered her with one finger and followed it with another and moved in a continuation of the dance beat they'd moved to earlier. Alex came in a sudden moment of violence, her hands tightly gripping Mitch's shoulders. Mitch leaned over her to kiss her gently again. She looked into Alex's eyes. "Thank you," Mitch said, "for giving me so much."

Alex shook her head. "No, I should be thanking you," she said. "And I'm hungry for more. You're not one and done, are you?"

Mitch responded with a hard kiss. "No. I can go as long as you want me to." And then she'd sleep like a baby, and there wouldn't be any drama when the sun rose.

CHAPTER THREE

"HELENE, HAVE YOU GOT time for coffee this morning, whenever you're ready?" Jessica leaned back in the chair at her desk and held her phone out in front of her. "I'm leaving for Minabo at ten, but it would be good to see you before I go."

"Certainement," Helene said. "I will get to you around eight, but I may be early."

Jessica rolled her eyes. Helene was always late and arrived out of breath with the story of some misadventure. "I really do have to leave at ten or I'll miss my flight, so please be early." After putting her cell down, Jessica called Earl in. "I have until eight to sign the last papers. Come and guide me through what you need." She patted the chair beside her.

"Yes, Madam Ambassador. I've organized all you need to finish. We've written the address you'll give at the Embassy reception and the one to the European Economic Community Trade Commission the following morning. You should look them over now to ensure you're comfortable with them."

"Right." Jessica leaned back and read through both pages. "These look fine. I assume you know exactly what they need to hear, and I'm just saying it?"

"Yes, ma'am, the reception is for military attachés in London and will be about the need for strong military representation across the world. The trade commission is highlighting the commerce between the US and Europe and the need for our partnerships to continue."

"Good," Jessica said. "They look okay to me. I'll sign off on them."

"We also have the usual email that requires your initials."

"Any invitations?" Jessica signed the papers, hardly reading most of them. She'd trusted Earl for years; he'd never put anything in front of her that wasn't in keeping with her political ideals.

"Yes, ma'am. The royal box at Wimbledon is the highlight, although there are several lunches and dinners as well, including one at Buckingham Palace. There are also a couple of receptions at different embassies and one at Goldman Sachs. I've put them all in your diary; the list is here."

"Thank you. I'll look it over on the plane."

"That's everything. I've put all the paperwork you need for your holiday in this folder. It includes the guidebooks and maps we've looked at over the past weeks. Your passport and tickets, along with the itinerary, are in the red inset."

"Thank you. Let's hope it all turns out well, and I get to see the gorillas. Can you see that my cases are brought down and put in the vestibule for when Greg brings the car around, please?" Jessica stood, her thoughts moving almost too fast to keep up with. "I'm having coffee with Helene Gaspar, the wife of the French ambassador. She's arriving shortly. I'll be in the garden room."

"Certainly, ma'am," Earl said and left the room quietly.

Jessica made her way from the office to the garden room, taking in everything she could about Winfield House, one of the most famous Ambassador's Residences in the world. Near Regents Park in Central London, it covered twelve acres, and successive ambassadors had outdone each other with their additions, adding priceless antiques and pictures over the years. Her husband, George, had been responsible for putting their mark on the place, and it suited them...but it still missed his presence. She shook off the maudlin thoughts and popped into the restroom to check her hair and makeup. Her hair didn't have any wayward strands escaping from the bun, but she needed a little touch of lipstick. She opened her Louboutin leather purse and redid her lips before adjusting her pink midi dress.

Once in the garden room, she sat in her favorite chair with a marvelous view through the several elongated windows across the grounds. The morning sunshine slid across the glass, leaving a crisscross pattern of shadows on the carpet next to her.

"Madam Ambassador. I have Madame Helene Gaspar with me. Shall I bring coffee?" James, her butler asked.

"Yes, please. Good morning, Helene. I expect you're pleased to escape for a few minutes?" Jessica air-kissed Helene three times and gestured for her to take a seat.

"Yes, Luc has a big meeting at the embassy, and it seems that half of France is attending. We have a dinner in our house in Kensington Palace Gardens this evening, and it will be the biggest we've held. So it's good to be able to slip away for a moment. Once I get back, I'll be busy until I get to sleep tonight." Helene waved vaguely toward the garden. "I want it to be perfect.'

"Have you bought a new dress?" Jessica asked.

"I took your advice and looked at some of the Gucc dresses and found cne that was très jolie. I love it. It's black silk and lace, and it's floor-length. Perfect," Helene said.

"I found this just in at Harvey Nichols and decided to celebrate going on holiday. It's stylish and comfortable, and I think I look fabulous." Jessica stood and twirled her dress.

"It's lovely. Now, you did take my advice to pack plenty of ordinary clothes to take with you, yes? Luc has visited several of those African countries, and while we enjoyed them, you have to take care. You never know what could happen." Helene placed her hand over Jessica's, her expression showing genuine concern.

"I know. You've reminded me more than once; I need to dress cheap, keep to myself, and don't stand out. Don't throw money around, and don't take any risks." Jessica thought that Helene was being a little over-protective. She could take care of herself, and there had been no trouble when other people went there to visit the gorillas. It was a properly organized small tour with only three people, and she expected to be well looked after. She didn't want a bodyguard, and it was only in certain countries that the US thought them necessary. So, the embassy agreed she could travel alone as long as it was with a company they agreed to.

"Chérie, I apologize," Helene said. "I did not mean to tell you what to do. I sound like my maman, giving instructions. It was done with the best intentions."

"I know that, of course." Jessica patted Helene's knee. "It's what friends are for. Now tell me about Wimbledon. Have you had an invite? If not, I expect I'll have a plus one for the royal box, and we can go together. It will be good if we get to see some of the stars, like Alcaraz or Djokovic."

"Even if Luc gets an invitation, I expect him to turn it down. He finds tennis so boring. So, when you get to it, yes, please. We can have a, how you say, girls' day out."

"Thank you, James," Jessica said as he brought in their coffee and chocolate cookies. He served them both and left the room. "When I get back from Minabo, we need to sort out when we can go to London Fashion Week. I can't wait to see the latest fashions. I'd love to go to Milan; I hope Carla can get us tickets so that we can all go."

"It's good that we have your contacts in London, Carla's in Italy, and mine in Paris. Luc is happier when I'm not underfoot," Helene said. "He needs me to be the perfect hostess, a beautiful woman, and a good lover. And when I do those things, he's putty in my hands when it comes to getting what I want."

Jessica did her best not to wince at the outdated notion. It wasn't her place to say anything, and it wasn't like she had so many friends that she could afford to upset this one. "George was a wonderful lover, and he introduced me to all the right people, as well as helping me learn how to talk to the types of people I'd never been around. He was a perfect mentor, but I managed to get this ambassadorship on my own merits. I'm quite proud of that, really." At the slight frown beginning between Helene's brows, Jessica back-pedaled. "And let's face it, we've had so much fun so far. It's wonderful that all of us have ended up in London."

Helene took a sip of her coffee. "It has been a few special years. It's a shame you have to do the ambassador things and can't have all the fun us wives have."

Jessica was actually glad for the respite from her social calendar that work provided. "I don't mind. I'm good at speeches, and I've got Earl to sort out what point I need to make and what I should say. As you know, I don't have much interest in the world, its events and happenings. Nothing changes. Everything stays the same. Why bother with getting to know this situation or that one? It will just change tomorrow." She shook her head and shrugged. "I know when I give my speeches that I don't say anything of substance, but I also know that no one is really listening. I've had a few people convinced that I should have a viewpoint. I can say honestly, I'm not an expert, and I'm not committed either way." She drank down the last of her coffee, thinking that she sounded jaded. It was true, though. This was a job like any other, just with better perks and more travel options. In the end, few people knew her name or cared what she did. It left her with a sense of ennui, which she buried under bags full of new clothes.

"I'm afraid I have to throw you out; I need to get myself ready. I expect the car to be here in a few minutes," Jessica said as she stood.

Helene hugged her lightly. "Enjoy your holiday. I'm sure you'll have fun. See you back here soon."

Jessica walked to the front door with her and watched Helene leave in her black limo. She needed to get going, her own limo would be ready soon enough. She hadn't had a complete break on her own since George died three years ago, and she was looking forward to having a holiday alone. She'd gotten used to going to functions without a plus one, but this was different; she was going to be on her own in a new setting. She would need to give an impression of confidence to the outside world and show that any sadness of being alone was of no matter, despite the inner reality.

* * *

The plane landed at Solunwa airport at seven in the evening, and Jessica had enjoyed her flight. It certainly helped to be able to travel first class with all the trappings of luxury that she enjoyed. The champagne was perfect, as was the excellent food she'd consumed while she'd read. She'd even managed a short sleep, so she was quite refreshed when the plane touched down. The air outside was hot and cloying, and the scent of plane fuel and overheated earth made her a little queasy. She collected her luggage and headed into the arrival hall, where the air conditioning was having little effect against the heat coming in through the open doors.

The noise of people shouting to get passengers' attention, directing passengers toward taxis, and the general melee of people found in any airport created a cacophony of sound. She looked around the sea of faces holding up boards and found the owner of the Big Country Tours sign. It was her personal tour guide, Jono Mbenwe, whom she'd spoken to on Zoom before traveling, so she was comfortable with him collecting her and ensuring her safety in lieu of an official bodyguard.

She'd tried to upgrade her hotel room when she'd booked, but she'd been told they were at capacity, although Jessica wondered how a top hotel could only cost $250 for the night. She had to hope it would be luxurious enough for her tastes. The drive there from the airport was on a brand new, two-lane expressway with very little traffic, and it took them straight into the tourist part of Solunwa. There was little to see, apart from billboards and several half-built buildings with cranes leaning over them imperiously. It was odd to see so few people after the mayhem in the airport.

The hotel wouldn't have looked out of place somewhere in Florida on the coast. It was clean and modern, and she found her room adequate for the one night. The tour company had emphasized that later accommodation would be much less luxurious. Jessica smiled and thought of Helene as she unpacked her very plain, pale green safari kit ready for the morning. Jono had said they'd be leaving at ten the next morning, and she couldn't wait to set off. If only George had been there to share it with her...

She shook off the melancholy and got into bed with the itinerary. The first stop was Princess Victoria National Park before two days on safari, aiming to see the "Big Five." She'd been unaware of who exactly the Big Five were before researching this trip and found out that it meant the elephants, leopards, lions, rhinos, and buffaloes. To be able to see the animals in their own habitat and spend time learning about them was going to be a perfect holiday. It would have been more perfect with George there, of course, but she'd promised him she'd keep the adventure going after he passed, and she was determined to do her best.

She woke early the next morning, ready for her big day, and headed down to the hotel lobby.

"Ma'am, are you ready to leave?" Jono asked. "Do you have your small suitcase as we have discussed?"

"Yes, I've packed what I think I'll need. I've been careful," Jessica said. "The hotel put my big suitcase into storage for me."

"Good, we're taking Mr. Frank Cotton and his wife, Hilary Cotton, with us. I'll introduce you once I've put your bag in the game cruiser."

"Is that them over there?" Jessica pointed to an older couple sitting in the foyer, looking at her and Jono.

Jono nodded.

"I'll go over and say hello," Jessica said. She strode over, pulling on her ambassador persona to bring out her inner confidence. "Good morning. It looks like we'll be traveling together. I'm Jessica."

The white-haired, distinguished-looking man with a moustache stood to shake hands and introduced himself and his wife. "We've come from Sydney. We're visiting some places we've always wanted to see before we get too old, and this trip has been top of the list for a long time."

Hilary also stood and shook her hand. "Where've you come

from?"

"I'm originally from Boston, although I've been working in London for a couple of years. Like you, I have a number of places I want to visit, and this is one of them."

Jono approached. "Luggage is loaded. Are you all ready? Let's get ourselves into the cruiser. Frank and Hilary, if we start with you on the raised seats in the back, and Jessica, you can sit up front with me."

The three travelers got themselves into the vehicle, with Frank and Hilary taking time to get settled. They were probably in their late seventies and undoubtedly, this tour would be difficult for them. She took photos of everyone on her phone, thinking they'd make a good start to the photos she wanted as a record of the journey. There wasn't much that interested her these days other than her social life, but this trip had re-energized her. Already she felt like she was free in a way she hadn't been in a very long time.

Jono gave them all a full water bottle. "There's a container in the back, so we have plenty of water when you need a refill." He climbed into the driving seat. "Today is about traveling from here to Princess Victoria National Park. We'll skirt the lake for part of the journey and head on using one of the main roads through central Minabo. It will take us much of the day, but we'll stop for breaks, and we'll have lunch in a white rhino sanctuary on the way. We'll look out for a variety of wildlife during our travels so you can take lots of pictures. Any questions?"

Jessica shook her head. She wanted to get the day underway. Her insides were vibrating, and a giggle bubbled up from nowhere. She hadn't been this excited since she was a child. She made herself lean back in her seat and let the energy of the day flow over her.

After the quiet journey from the airport, the road out of Solunwa surprised her. On reflection, she hadn't considered that the population had to live somewhere. The city was large and packed with people and cars, vans, and trucks. The vehicles were mostly heavily laden with goods of all kinds.

Moving slowly beside them was a trailer loaded with live chickens, tied and hanging upside down on the trailer sides. She blanched and turned away, only to see a horned cow with all its legs tied together on a rack on the back of a motorbike. It appeared to be used to it, because it lay there quietly. Her breathing hitched, and she swallowed hard. Jessica started to take a photograph but decided that it was an image that had been imprinted in her mind, and she'd never forget it. No one else needed that awful image.

Outside the city was mainly fields and low-lying land that Jono told them had often flooded in recent times, and the farmers lived with little money. Most of the crops were cash crops of tea, coffee, and sugar They only farmed small parcels of land and grew enough to feed themselves and make just enough profit to keep them from starving until the next harvest.

Due to the heat and the endless fields, Jessica had begun to doze off when a white SUV pulled out of a dirt road in front of them. Jono braked sharply, slamming Jessica against her seatbelt. *That's going to leave a bruise.* She peered through the windshield to get a closer look at the vehicle, which had effectively blocked the road.

Three men climbed out dressed in army camouflage with black balaclavas over their heads, all carrying some kind of machine guns. Two of them ran at their little tour bus, firing over the top of the vehicle into the distance. Jessica froze, and everything moved in slow motion. She opened her mouth to scream, but no sound came out. She could hear Hilary behind her shouting, and Frank calling out, "No, no, no," as the armed men got closer. Two of the men pointed their guns at Jessica and Jono, one on each side of the cruiser. The one on Jono's side barked at him to get out.

He turned to Jessica, looking panicked. "Whatever happens, the company will realize there's a problem if we don't—"

The man yanked the door open and grabbed Jono by his shirt to pull him out of the car. Something was said in a local dialect, and he hit Jono in the face with the butt of his gun. The man on Jessica's side banged the window with his rifle and demanded that she get out. She picked up her purse and tried to pull it over her shoulder as she climbed out of the car. It was silly, really, but she couldn't just leave the car without ID. The man pulled her purse from her and took out her wallet. He pocketed the money, then tipped the rest of the contents onto the ground before throwing her bag into the undergrowth. He grabbed her arm and dragged her forward, before pushing her into their SUV. Then he went back, and there was the sound of a single shot.

Jessica screamed, her terror finally let loose.

They'd shot Jono.

The Australian couple were still sitting in the back of the game cruiser, and she could hear their screams. They were still alive. But for how long? Why weren't they being taken as hostages too?

"Come with us, Mrs. Ambassador. We are taking you on a trip into our country," said the man who appeared to be in charge as he dragged her into the back of their Land Cruiser. He sat her down in the middle of the back seat and tied her hands in front of her with a piece of cloth. "We have a long drive, and we won't cover your face or gag you unless you cause us trouble. We want you to see our land and learn."

Thoughts, slow and sluggish, made it through her fear. "You know I'm an ambassador. I'm sure you'll be able to negotiate a lot of money for my release." A flicker of hope began in her chest, only to be snuffed out when he looked at her.

"If that was what we wanted to do, we would have taken the couple in the back as well," he said. "But we've left them. They have water, and they'll be found soon enough and taken to safety." He gave an order to the driver in another language, and they pulled away.

What on earth had she been caught up in? If they didn't want money, what did they want? Icy fear slid down her spine, making her shiver in the sweltering heat. It took everything in her not to imagine the possibilities. *Survive.* For the moment, that had to be her only focus.

CHAPTER FOUR

Alex sighed right down to the tip of her toes. As she walked along the road toward her flat in the early morning light after a night of sex like she'd never had before, she wondered if she should've stayed longer instead of leaving like a thief in the night. Mitch had been exactly what she'd needed, even though she wasn't the sort of woman she was usually attracted to. She preferred a woman who was much daintier and, while not necessarily a femme, someone with more feminine attributes.

Mitch was all muscle and movement, and there was nothing dainty or feminine about her. She was butch and blatant with both her haircut and dress. But Alex didn't regret last night for a single second. She sighed again. Life was like that right now. Whenever anything extraordinary came toward her, it somehow disappeared like frost on a summer day. A relationship with a woman that she would've gladly seen again and again wasn't meant to be. Instead, she'd find a project that she really wanted, and the bosses would say she wasn't qualified or some such. At what point, would things start going her way?

Back in her apartment, she showered and regretted once again leaving Mitch without so much as a note or her number. Even if Mitch wanted to get in touch, she couldn't. Alex dressed with half her mind on her clothes and the other half on those standout moments with Mitch leaning over her, and by the time she walked to her office, she was lusting after her again. *Stupid*. It was one night. They'd both gotten what they wanted from it, and it was time to move on. With a deep breath, she steadied herself and focused on the day ahead.

She stopped at the coffee shop and arrived in the office with two cups in hand.

"Oh, good, you're here. Thanks for this," Mary said as she took the coffee. "My turn tomorrow if you're here. The general wants to see you. The American Ambassador to the UK has been kidnapped while on holiday in Minabo."

Alex shrugged back into the jacket she'd been about to place on her chair.

"The whole of the Foreign Office, the American Embassy, and the White House want solutions yesterday," Mary said.

"Okay, I'm off." She headed out to see Edward Moss, the boss of Department 6. He'd been a general once, and he still sounded like one, with a lot of loud noise and bullshit. He ran D6 with a keen and intelligent mind in a department dedicated to rescuing women in dangerous situations around the world. Their operations were kept quiet or off the books altogether, and all knowledge of them was denied by the political commissars.

Alex tapped on his door. Her palms sweaty and her breathing rapid, and she could only hope this was the chance she'd been waiting for. *Please don't pass me by again.*

"Come," he said.

He sat at his leather-topped desk, in his shirt, habitual suspenders, and his tie depicting the Special Air Service, which was his old army regiment. His unruly blond hair looked more unkempt than usual, as if he'd been running his hands through it. "Morning, Alex. Did Mary tell you the news?"

"Yes, sir. What's the story?" Alex hadn't been invited to sit, so she stood awkwardly in the middle of the room.

"As far as I can tell, Jessica Landen, the US Ambassador to the UK, was taking a holiday to Minabo. She didn't want a lot of fuss and bother, and she didn't want any friends or staff accompanying her. Neither did she want any protection. She insisted it was a private visit. And because Minabo has seen little trouble in the last few years and wasn't on any warning lists, the US Embassy agreed she could go. She no sooner landed near a safari park than she was abducted at gunpoint. Her guide was killed, and two fellow travelers, an older couple from Australia, were left traumatized and abandoned but unharmed otherwise. Clearly, the ambassador was the primary target."

"And no one had any intelligence about problems in Minabo?" Alex asked.

"Politically, no one considered it an issue, so there seemed to be little risk. The UK and the US give a great deal of aid to the country, and the Minabo government wouldn't risk losing the aid or having sanctions made against them," Moss said.

"Do we know how long ago this happened? Knowing Africa, it could take days or weeks before news like this is released." Alex's mind was already spinning out possibilities.

"Three or four days, we think, according to the Australians." Moss ran his hands through his hair again, making it stand up in more bizarre tufts. "The Americans have spoken to the Minabo government, who are doing everything they can, but they have no embassy in Minabo and want to push for action. They've requested our assistance. It hasn't been released to the press yet, and they're hoping to keep it that way."

"We should send a team," Alex said. "I worry that she could be smuggled out of the country, which would give us problems. The Sudan is still struggling, as are the other surrounding nations, and a kidnapped ambassador could be lucrative business."

"I spoke to David Lawrence, the Deputy Chief of Mission at the US Embassy this morning. Ambassador Jessica Landen is a personal friend of the president, so they're insisting that the operation has US input. Ideally, they want to lead with a CIA-sponsored black ops team." Moss shook his head. "They don't have any African experts on staff in Europe. It's ludicrous, and I told him so We're going to lead, and they can provide a team."

This op had her name on it. She'd worked for years in Africa and spoke Swahili fluently. She ran in diplomatic circles and understood the nuances of politics and money in the continent. Flick had said a job would eventually happen. This was it, and she'd grab the chance with both hands.

"Which is the long way round of me telling you that you'll be leading a team of Americans to rescue Jessica Landen. You'll need to use every piece of diplomacy you have in your dealings with the US team and the Minabo government to get her out unharmed and with as little violence and loss of life as possible," Moss said. "We don't want the press to get wind of this either."

"Yes, sir." Her heart hammered in her chest, and she itched to dash from the office to get started.

"I want you to go over to the Minabo desk in the Ministry and get a full briefing. I made you an appointment for 1100 hours. I need you back here by 1400 hours for another discussion before we meet up with the US team."

"Do we know who's heading them up?" Alex knew one or two of the people at the US Embassy from her rounds of the various cocktail parties.

"Not yet," he said and made a note on his blotter. "You'll be leaving as soon as we have names confirmed and can get flights. I'll set Mary on that."

"Okay, sir, I'll pack my case and be ready to go whenever you say."

"This is important, Alex. Be careful and get the job done," he said and waved her off.

She closed the door behind her softly. This was her chance to prove herself, and nothing and no one would get in her way.

CHAPTER FIVE

MITCH LAY BACK IN the comfortable bed, smiling and thinking about the night before, putting it into her memory banks for some night when she was feeling particularly lonely. She got out of bed completely naked and made coffee with the makings from the complimentary tray. It was English coffee and a bit too strong for her, but she'd endured worse. Her cellphone rang, which was unusual, since she rarely talked to anyone on the phone. She lived her life by text. "Hello, boss. You checking up on me? I'm in my hotel room in my own bed." She sat back on the bed and sipped her coffee. "Alone."

"Too much information, Mitch," Paddy said. "Change of plan for the next few days. The ambassador you met earlier this week has been kidnapped in Minabo. You'll be flying there with the Brits and using our in-country assets to negotiate or facilitate her release."

"What about my operation in Mexico? We were just starting to get results." Tension began to knot her shoulders.

"Henri can take it over until you come back. She knows all the details," Paddy said. "I need my best person on this, Mitch. Go straight to the embassy this morning and speak to the Deputy Chief of Mission, David Lawrence. He'll brief you at midday. Good luck. See you when you get back."

"Yes sir." *Damn it all.* There was no point in arguing, but this was far from what she needed right now.

"And one last thing, Mitch. Think before you act, and you'll do fine. I'm counting on you," Paddy said.

He hung up, and she flopped back on the bed. *Shit.* Good thing she'd enjoyed a hot night with a hot woman. That would likely be the last time for a while. With a sigh, she jumped off the bed and headed for a shower. *Stop thinking. Start doing.*

It was just before 1500 hours when Mitch arrived at an unremarkable building near Sloane Square. It was an expensive area of London, and the building looked as if it had stood there for several hundred years without acknowledging the passing of time. Her trip to see David Lawrence had been less than useful as well as brief. He gave her what information he had, told her the ambassador was a good friend of the president's, and that there'd be a Brit leading the mission, which seemed weird and unnecessary. But he said they needed a military operation to find the ambassador, with a quick extraction to get her home again quickly. In and out like a fine needle in an embroidery. Something the British were better at, apparently. Now she sat waiting for her meeting with the agent who'd lead the team into Africa. God, she hated waiting.

"Lieutenant Brennan?" a woman asked as she came out of a back office. "I'm Mary. If you'd like to follow me, I'll take you up for the briefing."

The inside of the building was just as Mitch had imagined from the outside. Highly shined dark floors with the pervading smell of polish throughout. The walls were pale green and had large paintings that were lit from above to make the dark foyer lighter. As she walked past, she looked at one of the paintings. Something to do with a famous naval battle with wooden ships under sail. One of the Brits' victories, she expected. In some respects, she was slightly jealous of such a deep history, but in others, she was happy being from the US and having the flexibility that a shorter history allowed. She understood the Brits could be slow in making decisions, hampered by the fact that they often based them on the way they'd always done things. She would definitely chafe under the directions of the man running this operation and would likely have to take charge. Whatever. She'd do what she had to do to get things done.

Mary led her to a door and opened it, before ushering her in. The room had a large map on the far wall, and there were three men and one woman around a table in the middle.

The woman turned around, and Mitch's stomach dropped. *Alex.* She did her best to keep her expression neutral. Was *she* going to lead the mission? Two of the men looked like they were too old; one of them had eyebrows like gray bushes in a field of wrinkles. The younger guy had the gray pallor and glasses of a money man.

"Good afternoon, Lieutenant Brennan. May we call you Mitch?" asked one of the old guys with blond hair.

"Yes, sir, I'd prefer it." She took a seat at the table, making every effort not to look Alex in the eye. She'd *definitely* say something inappropriate if she did.

"I'm Edward Moss, the Head of Department 6, and the man sitting next to you is Mr. Jeffers, our financial whiz. The man sitting next to him is Noel Clarke, the minister with oversight of Department 6, and opposite you is the leader of this operation, Agent Alex Hartley."

Mitch nodded to each of them in turn. Alex looked at the file in front of her, her hands smoothing it like it had creases.

"So, Mitch, we're all ears," Moss said. "Would you like to tell us your thoughts on the operation?"

"I only know a little about Minabo. I've been at a security conference here in London, and I was pulled from it this morning. David Lawrence asked me to join you and find the ambassador. His office gave me details about some assets we can use in the country." Mitch glanced at Alex, but she still didn't make eye contact. "I assume I was selected because of my background in moving through unknown and possibly hazardous countryside and leading a team to give an armed response if necessary."

Finally, Alex looked up and her expression said everything Mitch was thinking. She was heading into an operation, and her briefing had been subpar. She was clearly unimpressed.

"Well, we can certainly improve your briefing," Moss said. "Can you tell us more of what you've been doing these last few years, Mitch? Obviously only the broad details. It will help us understand your particular skillset."

"I've been working on the Mexican border in the realms of people and drug-smuggling. We've had some good successes taking down cartels and coyotes. I work for a number of departments in my role, including the CIA, the DEA, Customs, the local police departments, and Border Patrol, of course." She hoped the bitterness at not being allowed to finish out the last big score on that project didn't come through in her tone.

Moss nodded like he understood something she'd missed. "Alex will tell you more as you get together about the details of what she proposes, but she's the operations manager for D6 and decides on the projects and operations we take on. I decided Alex should lead this project because she has extensive experience in Africa, both undercover and in a diplomatic role. She speaks fluent Swahili and has a sound knowledge of the African geopolitical landscape when it comes to economic and government arguments." He tilted his head slightly as he looked at Mitch, like he was analyzing her. "And that's important to both our governments, as you may realize. We both provide a lot of aid to that area, so it's a delicate dance, and you need to step carefully. We need you to be the consummate diplomat, even though you may be used to a more... physical response." He finally looked away to glance at the others at the table. "And of course, you'll need to maneuver around the president, who will need regular updates. I hope that you'll be able to provide backup for Alex and ensure this all runs smoothly."

"Of course, sir. We'll handle any threat quickly and silently." Mitch didn't usually *sir* everybody, but this was like being in one of those dramas on BBC America. Their posh voices and the way they dressed made it seem like they needed a *sir* from her. At this point, she'd probably even call Alex sir.

Alex scowled at her. "We're planning a *diplomatic* response in the first instance, so we won't be looking for an armed response unless all else fails. We'd like to think we can resolve this without a shot being fired. Minabo has a well-trained and efficient army, and I'd hope that if it's terrorists looking for money, they will step in." She tapped the table with her pen hard enough to make the plastic crack. 'You're there for worst-case scenario options, and if you can't be diplomatic and help in a more cerebral way, then I hope you can stay in the background and not make things worse."

Anger, hot and itchy, flooded her. Who the hell did Alex think she was? Mitch never played so close to home with her women and rarely found someone she'd want to spend more time with. Clearly, she wasn't going to have to worry about wanting to spend more time with Alex in the future. She'd already decided they were going to tiptoe around Africa like ballet dancers and that Mitch was just a muscled buffoon. Well, that wasn't Mitch. She'd just have to wait it out, and when they got to Minabo, she'd see the lay of the land and take over. They needed quick results if they were going to save Jessica Landen, and that didn't mean talking to some government ministers in Minabo in the pay of other governments. It meant showing them who had the upper hand and who could get results.

CHAPTER SIX

THEY KILLED JONO. THE sound of the gunshot continued to reverberate in Jessica's brain. He'd been kind, and his smile had been so sweet. The fear in his eyes had been so real... What was happening? These men knew what they wanted and were going to make sure they got it. She'd be next. They just needed to get the money for her release. Once they had it, they'd kill her. She'd read about this happening elsewhere in Africa, and perhaps it was her turn. The policy of not dealing with terrorists would apply here. She choked back tears, not wanting to let them see her cry.

The men who were with her talked around her as if this an everyday occurrence. She needed to pee but didn't know the word her captors would understand so tried "toilet." They'd ignored her. She waited a while but began to squirm, crossing her legs and motioning toward the outside. They stopped the SUV, and the young Black man sitting in front of her got out. He had big eyes, and his hair was cut short at the sides and unruly on top. He wore a Crystal Palace Football Club T-shirt and well-worn jeans. He opened her door and gestured. She stood in front of him, and he waved his machine gun.

"Here," he said. "You, go now."

Jessica suddenly understood what someone meant when they said they died of embarrassment. She had to go, and they weren't going to turn away. She burst into tears, although it probably achieved nothing. She undid her pants, counting for some reason, as if that would take away the indignity. She pulled them and her panties down from behind her so that she bared as little flesh as possible and squatted as directed. Of course, nothing happened.

No, she had to go now. She couldn't do this all for nothing.

The man with the gun pushed it against her head. She'd never been so scared. That got things moving and within moments, it was over with. The physical relief was worth the moment of humiliation. She stood up, pulling up her clothes as she did so. The men in the car jeered and laughed. Jessica chose not to react. Instead, she simply turned and got back in the car.

She had no earthly idea where she was. The safari park was in the west of the country, and the route they'd taken had no direction posts. The roads had started out as single-lane tarmac and had soon changed to dirt roads, often no wider than the SUV and almost becoming the savannah on either side. As the journey continued, Jessica dozed as best she could to block out the terror, but the road was full of potholes and flooded portions that jarred her back into the nightmare. It was worse than being on an uncontrolled fairground ride, and Jessica's nausea kept rising. It was all she could do to keep whatever was left in her stomach down. It made her seat in the back both uncomfortable and almost painful, and whenever she stopped to think, she started crying again. For the most part, they simply ignored her, for which she was deeply grateful.

Eventually the car stopped near a set of round huts that had grass roofs and hard mud walls. There were a couple of huts with rusty, corrugated iron roofs and concrete walls, which had clearly been fixed here and there with hard-packed mud. Her heart raced as she watched the people get up and stare at the SUV. She was hot and dirty, thirsty and hungry, and her thoughts of the future were terrifying. A fresh bout of tears would likely smear away the last of her makeup, making her look as wretched as she felt.

An older man with graying hair stood under a grass overhang, clearly meant for simple gatherings in the shade. The driver got out of the car and went over to him. The other men got out of the car, and one gestured for her to get out. She inched her way out, her body stiff after spending most of the day huddled in the back of the car in a state of fright. She leaned against the car and looked around her. It was just a village like any other, with children running around and the adults watching with wary curiosity. No one seemed sympathetic or inclined to help.

The older man came over to her. "Good evening, Ambassador Jessica Landen. I am Mukasa Bitalo. You may call me Chief. I welcome you to our village Ponba in the lands of Northern Minabo. This area we call Kakuku, which is the land of our forebears. It has witnessed all that has happened in our lands for thousands of years." His English was heavily accented but good.

"I expect that your forebears witnessed the death of my guide and my dehydration as well," Jessica said. Fear slowly gave way to rage, fire burning away ice and letting off steam.

"Our people's spirits live on in these lands and guide us while we live with the challenges of our day-to-day life," he said. "This is why you are here. We need you to help us."

"You didn't need to kidnap me and bring me all the way here. Why didn't you send me a message and ask?" She closed her eyes against her anger; she needed to be diplomatic.

"I have sent many messages to both your government and that of the United Kingdom, but we have had no response. We are now desperate, and your coming to Minabo to see it for yourself was a gift. Our prayers were answered by the spirits," he said. "There is a good reason you haven't had water. Please come with me, and I will get you food and drink, and you will meet some of my family."

Surrounded by the three men who'd captured her, Jessica could do nothing but obey. She followed the chief to the grass overhang from which he'd emerged, but only the man who'd leered over her as she peed came in with them. The other two stayed outside as if they were on guard, but whether that was against other armed men or to keep her from running away, Jessica was unsure. Where they expected her to run, she didn't know either.

"This is Joseph, my oldest son." He gestured to the man with them.

Joseph sneered at her with cold eyes. He was nowhere near as welcoming as his father seemed to want him to be. He had killed her guide without a thought, and Jessica understood he would do the same to her if she strayed from the path they had planned for her.

"This is my first wife, Lulu. She has prepared food for us," the chief said.

Lulu looked her up and down, and Jessica became conscious of how disheveled she was. Her tunic was lined with grime, and her pale lemon-colored shirt was patched with sweat. She'd sweated her makeup away, and her hair fell about her face. She probably couldn't have looked less like an ambassador if she'd tried. Lulu brought her a drink of water in a plastic tumbler, and she drank it down eagerly. She held out her hand. "May I have another one, please?" Jessica said.

Lulu poured her another one out of a large yellow, five-gallon container.

"You can drink the water here because we have a bore hole funded by money raised locally by a charity that uses profits from an annual cycling event for the local villages. The water is clean and plentiful," Mukasa said. "The aid money your country has sent to Minabo is supposed to fund this kind of thing, but it never gets here."

"Our government is corrupt, and we need the attention of the international press to show the world the unfairness." Joseph stomped across the hut and stood directly in front of his father, shouting something in their language. Mukasa put his hands on his son's shoulders and spoke quietly to him. Joseph stormed away.

"My son is impatient. He wants attention now. He wants all the wrongs against our people to be fixed quickly," he said, shaking his head. "I must also convince the younger generation that violence will not get them the results they wish for. Once you see our problems, you will understand why he feels the way he does."

"I know little about your way of life and your problems. I have no idea what you expect me to do." Jessica ground her teeth together, curbing her nausea. She clenched her hands into fists. "You're a villager somewhere in Africa, and I'm only one woman. If you kill me, you'll still be a villager in Africa, and the American public will turn against you. They certainly won't give you more aid."

"That is what I tell my son," he said. "And our efficient armed forces would quickly be everywhere, looking for people who are not happy with the government. It would hurt us in many ways."

Lulu turned from where she'd been working at a mud-baked stove and indicated that the food was ready. They sat on a rush mat on the ground, and Jessica was given a bowl of stew and some white rice on a green leaf with a vegetable that looked like spinach. She had no idea how to eat it without cutlery. Maybe she'd missed something.

"Follow what I do," the chief said.

He picked up some of the rice-like food in his hand and shaped it into about a dessert-spoon size, then he put some spinach in it and dipped the ball into the stew. She made a couple of attempts and managed to get some food. She couldn't say she liked any of it. The rice stuff tasted of nothing, and the spinach and stew were both highly spiced, and she didn't like either. But she ate nearly all of what she was told was ugale plus a little of the spinach and stew, recognizing that she had to eat to stay healthy. It was filling, if not tasty. She was given a tin mug of tea, which consisted of several different green leaves stewed in her mug. She was surprised when she found it refreshing, and though it wasn't the kind of tea she'd gotten used to in England, it was good enough.

The hurricane lamp provided a small cone of light as the sun set outside. Jessica had never used one; the pungent smell surprised her, as did the little light they actually gave. Lulu tapped her arm and made the sign for bed.

"You'll be sleeping with Lulu and some of the grandchildren," Mukasa said. "Go with her. She will show you the latrine. You may shower tomorrow morning. There isn't enough light now. Good night."

"If you would just let me go, I can send people to see about the water—"

He held up his hand. "Good night."

Jessica followed Lulu out of the hut to another one across the way. It had no sides at all, and she could see sleeping forms already settled in it. Lulu led her through a small patch of tall green plants that may have been some kind of corn.

They came upon a one-person-sized brick building with a canvas door. The smell told her it was the latrine. Lulu gave her the light, and Jessica was grateful for the moment of privacy, if nothing else. She stood on the concrete slab, lifted the lid with a long handle, and sighed. *It's not exactly a Japanese toilet*. She used it and replaced the lid, before picking up the lamp and returning to Lulu. The air, though still rank with stench, was better than it was behind the canvas wall. Lulu pointed to an area where she could wash her hands with a bar of soap and a small jug of water.

She followed Lulu back to the open hut, where she was shown a space on a rush mat, slightly separate from everyone else. Lulu handed her a thin blanket. It wasn't much, but she might be glad of it later as the air cooled. She was given her own mosquito net, and Lulu climbed under another beside the children.

The ground was hard, the noise of the children snuffling was something she wasn't used to, and she was sure they'd keep her awake. She almost smiled. She'd been kidnapped, forced halfway across Minabo at gunpoint, she'd eaten strange food with her fingers, and she was sleeping in a hut with no walls. But she was worried that the children would keep her awake. Her eyes watered, and she cried until she drifted to sleep.

* * *

She opened her eyes to see a young child staring at her, lying beside her outside the net. She couldn't help but smile when the child grinned at her. "Good morning."

The child giggled.

"Do you speak English?" Jessica asked.

"Manchester United."

Lulu came into the hut and spoke to the child, who jumped up and ran away.

The previous day flashed through Jessica's mind, cutting like glass, unwelcome and full of pain. The only way to survive this was to embrace the experience and stop wilting in fear. She was fit and healthy but as she sat up, she realized she was also too old to be sleeping on the floor. Everything ached.

Lulu gestured for Jessica to follow her. The two armed men from the day before were at the door of the hut. Although there were odd English words like rich and white woman, she couldn't make out the rest. They jostled her as they walked, making her lose her balance, and only Lulu kept her standing. Lulu spoke sharply to the men, and they slowly and reluctantly pulled back, resentment clear in their eyes. They all walked behind Lulu to the latrine in single file. The men went to follow her into the makeshift building, but Lulu shouted at them, and they froze in place.

Lulu handed her a brightly colored orange top and a piece of brown cotton, which she shook out and discovered was a long skirt. The shower was a jerrycan in a sort of shelter made from branches, leaves, and old clothing. The guards were out of sight so, despite gaps in the "walls," Jessica simply got on with it; she wanted to wash off the dirt and the memory of yesterday. She tipped the jerrycan over her and gasped at the cold water. She tried to get plenty in her hair, which had come out of the journey the worst. She scrubbed with the leaves Lulu had given her, and amazingly, they left her skin feeling fresh.

"Soap for hair," Lulu said in English and handed her a large bar of white household soap.

Who knew she'd be grateful for something so banal? She emptied the jerrycan over her head and finally felt clean. She had a freshness that she'd never felt before, standing here in the middle of nowhere, naked and essentially alone. Lulu handed her a small piece of towel, but the already rising temperature and low humidity dried her naturally.

She dressed in the clothes Lulu had given her, sans underwear—another strange feeling. She bundled her dirty clothes together and followed Lulu back to the village, where she put her dirty clothes in a pile by her sleeping area.

"Washing after tea and food," Lulu said.

"Thank you for looking after me." Jessica wasn't sure it was the right thing to say. Should she thank someone who was holding her captive?

"My husband and son shout at each other about you. I agree with my husband, we need you to help us." She smiled. "So, I help you. Come."

She followed Lulu to the food hut, where she stirred a pot on the mud stove before handing her a plate of something that looked like beignets, served with a bowl of peanuts. They were sweet and filling. She would have given anything for a coffee but was handed a cup of something else instead. It was creamy and spicy, and she recognized it as chai tea from her other travels. "How do you make this, Lulu?" Jessica asked.

"When I get up in the morning, I milk the cows with the other women, and we share the milk we collect. We cannot keep it for more than one day, so we use it all. A good breakfast drink is milk boiled on the stove until it is thick. We add tea and spices to make what you have."

"It's delicious. Thank you."

"We go to wash pots." Lulu collected the pots and pans from last night's meal as well as the breakfast pans.

Jessica, feeling like she should help and not just sit around waiting for things to make sense, carried two bowls in her arms, and they made a second trip for the rest. Weirdly, it felt good to take part in village life. Perhaps if she proved herself useful, they'd continue to treat her kindly. They left the bowls and pans to dry on a wooden stand made of branches, which was situated about three feet off the floor to keep it clear of dirt.

They got more water from the borehole tap in a collection of jerry cans and carried it to the huts. They washed the clothes by hand with cold water in a bowl and another large bar of soap. They rinsed the clothes and hung them to dry over the fences. Jessica wasn't sure she wanted to wear her safari suit again, because the clothing she wore now was much cooler in the heat of the day.

Later, Jessica watched Lulu make chapatis, with a selection of vegetables, cassava, sweet potatoes, and onions rolled inside. It'd been many years since Jessica had made food for herself, though initially she and George had learned together. She remembered evenings when they chopped and cooked, and shared stories of their days. The things she'd learned soon came back to her, and she fell into the rhythm of it easily.

"How many people are at this homestead?" Jessica asked.

"About one hundred. We have land around us, which we use for our cattle. The chief is thought to be wealthy because he has several hundred cattle. They are our main trade. He had to pay my father one hundred cattle for me when we were younger. He now has four wives, but he still has more cattle than anyone." Lulu straightened and smiled as she stared into the distance.

"Where do his other wives live?"

"Here. We each have our own fenced areas. I am his first wife and have been his wife for over thirty years, so I am like a business partner now. We spend time together working out the future. His other wives provide his creature comforts. And more children. I am done with that side of things," Lulu said and roared with laughter. "Sometimes having more wives can be useful for us too."

"Is your village similar to other villages in the grasslands?" Jessica asked, peeling cassava under instruction.

"No. It's different here. We are lucky because we have managed to get improvements. We are closer to the road and have enough money to pay for our children to use the school. We were given a borehole by a charity, and they helped us with the latrines, and the mud-baked stove. We also got help from an American Christian charity. The mosquito nets save our children from dying of disease and malaria. Others further into the savannah have not been so lucky."

"Has the charity helped everyone in the area?" Jessica asked.

"Many of the homesteads and villages across the grasslands do not have these facilities." Lulu sighed as she put more vegetables out. "They use water from streams or rivers that is dirty and even boiling it doesn't make it safe. They wash all their things in cow urine. You may think we are primitive—my son says we are compared to town dwellers—but we are modern against the other villages."

"Oh dear," Jessica said.

Lulu shook her head. "Western governments like yours have paid money to Minabo to help these people and the three quarters of the population who are struggling with disease and starvation. But we do not see it. We are helped by local and Christian charities, but the real aid money is just used to make money for the government. It makes me angry, but the chief will tell you more about it. It is why we went to such measures to get you here. We *need* you to tell our story. No one will listen to us."

"I don't understand. Doesn't my government check their money was well-spent? And withdraw funds if not? They must understand that you aren't getting the help you need." Jessica passed the pile of chopped onions to Lulu. She couldn't believe that governments got away with what was essentially theft.

"The US has no one in the country to check these things, and the government will take your money and say thank you to the American people. Then spend the dollars how they wish. Their wish is *never* to help the people."

Later that afternoon, while the women were sitting for the first time that day, the chief visited. Jessica ached and was glad for the respite. Where were the men when the women were sweating the day away?

"We will be leaving first thing tomorrow morning," Mukasa said. "I need to move my cattle across our land, and we will visit some other villages so you can see the way we live. We will take a game cruiser for some of it, but we will walk a lot of the way. I want you to see the grasslands across to the horizon."

Before she could ask what would happen if she didn't want to go, if she wanted to stay here, where it was safe with the other women, Joseph came to his father's side.

"Baba, we need to move more quickly. If the army finds out we have white lady here, they will kill us. But if we kill her, we show them we are not afraid and can make demands and will see results."

It was clear he was speaking in English to show her the nature of her position here. His two friends came over, and one of them shoved his weapon hard into Jessica's side. She cried out and jerked away. They were showing her how tenuous her life was, and it was only the chief that was keeping her alive. It was a terrifying thought.

Mukasa shouted in the Minabo language at the man, but he just muttered under his breath and gave her an unkind smile. Jessica prayed she'd never be left alone with him. Lulu came over and raised Jessica's shirt a little and pressed her hand to Jessica's side. She shook her head, gave her a gentle pat on the hip, and retreated.

"I'm sorry about my son and his friends. They are worried about the future. I will keep you safe, and it will be good if you cooperate," the chief said, moving away to sit in a nicely carved wooden chair.

The rest of the day disappeared with chores. Jessica collected the washing with Lulu and helped prepare the evening meal. Her side ached, but Lulu said nothing was broken, and she believed her. The pain was a good reminder not to get comfortable. These men were desperate and angry, and she was a captive, not a guest. Before it got dark, Lulu gave her a plastic bag to put her clothes in and presented her with a small piece of clean towel, a bar of soap, and a comb for the journey.

"Are you not coming with us?" Jessica asked. Fear, dulled a little by the quiet routine of the day, rose sharp and bitter in her throat.

"It is not my place. I run the homestead and do not travel away. The chief will look after you," Lulu said.

"I hope so. I'm sorry to say I don't trust your son and his friends." Jessica shivered at the thought of being alone anywhere with them.

"They are good boys, just impatient. I will speak to them this evening and remind them how to behave." Lulu didn't look overly confident.

"Thank you for all you've done to help me. You've made my time here less difficult than it could have been." It didn't hurt to show gratitude for even the smallest of kindnesses. And if she came back here, perhaps that bit of gratitude would help her make it home.

Beneath the mosquito net, she slept fitfully. In the village, she'd had a smidgen of security, thanks to Lulu. But once they left, she'd be alone with men who'd sooner kill her and use her as an example than try to enlist her help. Tears slid down her cheeks and onto the mat as the realization set in; there was a very good chance she would never make it home.

CHAPTER SEVEN

"W E LOOK FORWARD TO getting some good news soon," Moss said as he escorted the minister and Jeffers from the office.

Alex stared into space, her thoughts rapid and chaotic. The meeting had gone well, and the adrenaline was still awash in her body as she thought about the things she needed to do, like the detail mapping and any extra intelligence. The intelligence she most needed was about the American part of the operation which, so far, was just a bag full of promises and nothing concrete. And that brought her to Mitch, who sat opposite, clearly waiting for her to say something.

She'd looked at her on and off during the meeting, and all she could think about was the shape of her shoulders and the clear definition of her biceps against her shirt sleeves. Her sex was buzzing and wet; Mitch's body had given her a craving like she'd never had before. *Damn it*. She *never* mixed her personal and professional lives. Ever. She'd seen the disaster when other couples tried to mix things, and they often ended up straying because their ops were rarely at the same time and place. The strain eventually ripped the relationship into sad little shreds. She wasn't going to play that game with any woman, let alone one she was about to go on a dangerous mission with. No distractions. She cleared her throat but couldn't find any words to say.

Mitch pushed away from the table and stood. "I know today has been strange. I didn't expect the day to turn out as it has, and I'm sure that it's the same for you. Could we go somewhere quiet and talk things through?"

"Come to my office first," Alex said. "We need to discuss the details of the op and what I expect to happen. And I want the details of the manpower we have available."

Mitch's eyebrow twitched, and she motioned grandly toward the door. "After you."

Alex strode past, trying not to breathe in Mitch's cologne. She couldn't believe that Moss had cooked up some plan with the Americans that would use assets already on the ground in Minabo. She was aware of the American troops often allowing infantry and militia to retire in African states and then paying them a small retainer for the use of their services. It was a disaster waiting to happen, running an op with mercenaries who would only listen to Mitch. Where should she go from here? This op was starting out as a mess, and she suspected the rest of the op would follow along if she didn't get a strong handle on it. She'd only led a couple of ops on the ground from start to finish. She'd co-led many times, but she'd always been undercover. Flick had trained her personally several years ago, and she'd been out in the field several times to keep her skills valid. She was mostly confident in her ability, certainly with a UK-led and staffed op. But the Americans... Everyone knew they were cowboys who weren't good with boundaries.

Once at her office, she gestured for Mitch to sit. Alex took her own seat behind the desk, glad for the barrier between them. "We need to ensure we have all the information we require, so we can figure out possibilities for the op. Mary has been looking up detailed maps of the area, which she'll provide both online and in paper form. I'd like us to explore them and see where cities and safari parks fit together. I'd also like to see where there are pockets of unrest. Did your briefing provide you with any of that information?" Alex kept her eyes on the files in front of her rather than meet Mitch's eyes, which Alex could still only picture half-lidded with desire.

"No. There was little about Minabo, and the big info desks in the US are getting me more later today. I'll share that with you when I get it. I have a total of twenty men to draw on, although I think Mr. Lawrence was hoping it wouldn't come to that. He, like your bosses, is expecting us to solve the problem diplomatically."

Alex quelled the instant irritation that rose at Mitch's tone, which didn't suggest she thought much of that option. "I think we're *all* hoping that, but the government in Minabo has become a little unstable of late. They've removed the American Embassy, and it looks like they'll do the same to the UK. I don't know why they'd antagonize the countries giving them aid, but I have information that countries such as Russia and China are giving them railways and power stations and other help. I suspect that the diplomatic channels are going to be difficult."

"What are the Minabo government doing that's pissed some people off?"

"The country still has three quarters of its population without toilets and half the population is further than a half mile away from clean water." Alex read from the briefing Mary had left on her desk. "Given the poverty levels, it looks like the aid money isn't going where it's supposed to." She sighed and finally looked up "Please be circumspect in your discussions with locals, should you have any. We have no proof that the money isn't being used properly, and we don't need a political conflict."

Again, Mitch gave that slight grin and raised her eyebrow. "No problem. We'll try to behave ourselves, so we don't step on any delicate toes."

Alex ignored the unsubtle sarcasm. "The other problem in Minabo is that the northern savannah is mostly the home of a number of tribes. They've owned the land for many years and are cattle and subsistence farmers." She looked at her notes and pointed to an area on the map. "The cattle are their whole economy. They buy and sell everything using them, including their wives. The government has decided the tribes have too much land, so they've been offering them cash."

"And there the problems start," Mitch said. "It's a lot like what happened to the Native Americans: no cattle, no land, no crops, and no way to feed and house their wives and children. They know nothing else, so they're displaced." She shrugged. "It's a vicious circle that happens everywhere."

Alex leaned forward, her ire rising at Mitch's blasé attitude. "The ones that aren't selling are being told to fence their land; if it's fenced, they can keep it. Of course, therein lies another problem. How do you fence grasslands? They can only fence small areas and end up giving up their land by default. The government will take as much as they can grab, and the word is, they're going to use the land for running luxury safaris, the sort with big-game hunting."

Mitch grimaced. "Diplomacy. What a crock. This is more likely to be a smash and grab. And I can see why I've been picked to lead the US team. I'm good at thinking on my feet when an armed response is needed." She smiled. "We make a great team. We fit together beautifully." She flexed a bicep. "I'll be the brawn, and you can be the brain."

Alex blushed, the heat rising from her core to her hairline. "Where are your troops based?" Anything to take the attention away from her body, which seemed determined to undermine her professionalism. She was *not* going to have a personal relationship with Mitch. She had to maintain a working relationship only to get the job done well and prove she was capable out in the field. Clearly, she was going to have to keep repeating this to herself until her body accepted it. The faraway dream was love and a happily-ever-after with a cottage by the sea. And right now, she didn't want lust and sex taken in hot moments on the job.

Mitch was great for a night, but not for a lifetime. And now, she couldn't be good for a night either. *So be it.*

Mitch looked at her and pointed at the map. "The crew will have access to hang out at this town outside the capital. As I understand it, the leaders live here, along with one or two of the primary crew. The rest are spread around nearby, and they can call on them as needed. They're all experienced in armed conflict, because they're left over from a militia posted in the region five years ago. They've been there for so long, they've become experts in the political issues in that part of Africa. They also know a great deal about the surrounding countries. I don't know many of them personally, but I've read their files."

"Perhaps we should meet them when we arrive. We could probably learn a lot from them. They may have heard who took the ambassador." Alex studied Mitch's expression and noticed the lines tighten a little around her eyes.

"You want to come with me?" Mitch asked. "Okay, of course. Although I hadn't visualized that scenario."

"No? Why not?" Alex was in charge of this whole thing, and Mitch wanting to brief her team without Alex there would diminish any authority she might have with them. That was the bad vibe this op was bringing, all there in one move.

"I thought you'd be all diplomatic around the government, doing lots of talking and politicking, and with the best will in the world, I'm no diplomat." Mitch leaned back in her chair. "While you were doing that, I expected to go and make contact with the guys and brief them in case we needed them to move quick. We can cover more options if we work different people."

"I suppose that would make sense." It *was* sensible, but she needed to ensure she had control, and this was the area she could lose it. Then she'd just be another talking head surrounded by people who wanted to use guns instead of words. "But they should talk to me before making any decisions. We need to plan any op to ensure its success. Don't you agree, lieutenant?" She refused to wince at the peremptory tone coming out of her mouth. Mitch needed to know who was in charge.

"Yes, ma'am." Mitch's expression remained unchanged, and yet there was something that suggested she didn't, in fact, agree.

Mary entered Alex's office. "You're leaving on a direct flight from London at 0600 hours tomorrow, arriving at 1500 hours at Solunwa. I've sent details to your phones. You have extra luggage allowances as usual and will be able to collect hardware from the

British Embassy, although I'm sure your men will have their own supplies on the ground."

"Thank you for all your work on this." Mitch nodded to them both and stood. "I'll tell you about my briefing from the US on the flight. I need to make sure I have kit suitable for the environment." She turned and was gone.

Alex stared at the space where she'd been sitting, still thinking about the night and the way they'd melded together. They were so different, so ying and yang and yet, she couldn't help but feel like they'd get each other. That didn't matter though. As long as they got along well enough on the mission to complete it, they didn't need to have anything outside of that.

"Why do I think you haven't told me something?" Mary sat down and folded her arms. Her expression was serious, but there were the beginnings of a smile at the corners of her mouth. "The look the lieutenant was giving you would have burned a steak to a crisp. I saw you looking at her too when she was talking to the general. *You* were undressing her! It's the best meeting I've been to for months purely because I was trying to work out what was going on. You can't convince me you haven't met before. So spill."

"We met last night at the bar in town. We ended up in her hotel room." She rolled her eyes at Mary's faux look of surprise. "I left in the early hours, thinking about how special the night had been and wondering why my luck had run out. I met someone interesting and was expecting them to head back to America."

"Your luck didn't run out at all. In fact, it's all running your way," Mary said.

"But it isn't." Alex threw up her hands. "I've never done romance at work, and I don't want to start now. You and Mo have been together years, but you're the exception. Too many of our colleagues have ended relationships with cheating, one way or another. It's not worth it." She rested her head against the chair. "Not to mention we're about to go on a delicate mission, and she's got the diplomacy of a rhino on cocaine."

"The separation in the early years was hard for us, but we rode it out," Mary said. "And now Mo has become a contractor, so she can select her jobs, and I've got this desk job, we're like normal couples and see each other most evenings and weekends."

Alex tilted her head. That didn't sound so bad. But… "It's the constant separation that worries me. I don't want to be with someone who has to take off at a moment's notice. I want someone who'll be around, someone I can rely on. I don't need a woman who can't wait for the next op; she wouldn't be great wife material."

"Fair enough. You know what you want. Just don't forget, if you change your mind about her, you'll have to tell HR, so that they can do all the checks. Because she's not English, it's doubly important to tell them soon."

Trust Mary to think of the logistics of a romance. Alex fiddled with her pen. "So more than one night's sex is a notification requirement?'

"Maybe not quite so soon, but certainly three or four would be probable. It's all about what you might say in bed beyond the usual 'Yes, yes, yes,' and 'Oh Mitch, Oh Mitch, Oh Mitch.'" Mary laughed loudly. "Seriously though. You hold many national secrets, as does Mitch. It would become a sensitive situation."

"That just adds to all the reasons why I should stop things here and stay professional," Alex said. "Along with all the other reasons—not that I needed them."

"Good luck with that," Mary said. "The way you two were looking at each other, it's going to end in flames if you don't get together."

Alex's phone rang and she tried, unsuccessfully, to shoo Mary out of her office.

"Would you like to meet up for dinner tonight?" Mitch asked. "Have a final blow-out of good food…and catch up on you and me?"

"Well, I was going to sort out my pack—"

"You can do that first. I found a little Italian restaurant on Sloane

Street called Azzurra which I've been told does amazing fish. I could pick you up at eight. Will that give you enough time?"

"I'll see you at eight." Alex dropped the phone on her lap and stared at it.

"I am *not* going out with anyone I'm working with," Mary said, mimicking Alex's voice. Then she said, in Mitch's deeper tone, "Would you like dinner tonight?" She batted her eyelashes. "Ooh, yes, please."

Alex threw a wadded-up piece of paper at Mary's back as she scrambled from the room laughing. How was she supposed to keep her hands off Mitch if she struggled to refuse a simple dinner date? *It's just to set the record straight. I'll define my boundaries and tell her there won't be anything more between us, and that will be that.* She gently banged her forehead on the desk. Could it be that simple?

CHAPTER EIGHT

M ITCH SAT ACROSS THE table from Alex and grinned. This beautiful woman, who was whip smart, knew her own mind, and had a body that Mitch could sti l feel and taste, was having dinner with her. Alex had given so much of herself that, for the first time in her life Mitch wanted to spend more than one night with someone.

This morning, she was thinking about going back to the US after having lost touch with the best thing that had happened to her in ages. Now she was going to be with her for as long as the op lasted, and Mitch was wondering how things might work. No doubt the discussion would cover their relationship going forward, if one night's phantasmagoric sex was a relationship starter. Although, she had to admit that Alex's stiff, buttoned-up persona in the office earlier had set her teeth on edge, just a little. She wasn't great at taking orders from someone she didn't even work for. *Shit.* Technically Alex was her boss for this mission.

They ate a delicious meal which started as they chatted about the essentials they needed to pack and how bad the mosquitoes were. There was a long moment's silence.

"I think we should talk about last night." Alex stifled a cough, and her face flushed.

"Okay," Mitch said. "I'll start by saying it was fucking magnificent."

"It really was." Alex sighed. "But I just wanted you to know that we can't do this."

"Do what, exactly?" Heat coursed through her body. "Have dinner together? Set the room on fire with mind-blowing sex? Talk about climate change?" She leaned forward a little. "You might need to spell it out for me."

"Please don't lose it, Mitch. I just wanted us to talk through where we stand."

Mitch quelled her irritation. Several people glanced across at them from other tables. She sighed and motioned for Alex to continue.

"I had a wonderful night with you. When I left this morning, I was sad that one night was all we'd ever have because of your return to the US."

"I was thinking the same thing," Mitch said. "Then I decided there must be some luck involved when, of all the people in London, the only person I've ever wanted for more than a night was sitting right there at Department 6."

"Now you see the difficulty?"

"What difficulty?" Mitch shrugged. "I want more. I want to take you back to my hotel room for a repeat performance. I've been thinking about you all day, and I'm more than ready." That was an understatement. Her boxers and pants were too tight in all the wrong places. Or maybe all the right places. Either way, it didn't look like Alex was interested in revisiting their chemistry. "It isn't like I'm asking you to marry me or go rent a U-Haul tomorrow. It's just sex. Really, really great sex." She grinned, but Alex looked away.

"I need to keep my mind on the job we have to do. There are far too many difficulties when it comes to a relationship—or whatever we might have—with a military person from another country." Alex took a big swig of her scotch. "And I'm looking for someone permanent. Not someone for one moment."

"I get it. I want you in my bed again, but I accept that you're saying no. You want another?" Mitch smiled and slid her hand over Alex's.

"Yes to the scotch, but please don't do that." Alex pulled her hand away. "You said earlier today that you were used to thinking on your feet. Will you tell me more about that?"

Mitch clenched her jaw. "The world I work in is fluid. We never know what we're going to have to deal with or what we're going to find. Probably the same as you." She doubted it, somehow.

"True. We go to an address for a surprise raid and find that they got word we're coming, and it's a trap. That's happened more than once, you know the kind of thing...slack-mouthed informants or just plain traps." Alex's shoulders relaxed, and it was clear she felt on solid ground now.

"Yeah, we have that happen too." Maybe they did have more in common then. "Not to mention all the different agencies that are often involved. Makes it hard to get good intel. It happens much more than it should, which is why I like working alone, with a small team. We get shit done without all the red tape and communication issues."

"We don't have that issue, thank God. But we are dealing with situations across the world, so distance and lack of intel are real problems for us too." Alex looked at her intently. "Do the operations you go on affect you afterward?"

Mitch wasn't sure she wanted to have this discussion, and she probably shouldn't say anything at all. "It's the deaths I find hardest to deal with. Especially knowing that I've caused a few of them." That was enough, especially if Alex was going to be her boss. She didn't need some kind of psych concern coming at her from that side. "Do you have nightmares about some of the things you've seen and done?"

"A few, but I'm okay most of the time," Alex said, a distant look in her eyes. "If I get over-tired, I'm more likely to have one. Though I don't know why I'm telling you; even my best friend doesn't know that." She shook her head. "What about you?"

How to answer that without giving too much away? Mitch tossed back the last of her scotch. "Life on the border is mostly unlawful, and the person with the best strategy and biggest weapon is the one likely to win. I make sure that's always me."

"So why do you know so little about Africa and Minabo?"

"I focus on what I need to know. For years, that's been everything to do with cartel territory. Africa hasn't been on my radar. Perhaps we should have coffee if we're going to keep talking?" She pushed her glass away. "I don't want any more alcohol tonight."

"That's a good idea." Alex raised her eyebrow. "Though we will be leaving for our respective beds. Why didn't you get a proper briefing at the embassy?"

"I wondered that myself. Lawrence, our Deputy Chief of Mission, spent nearly thirty minutes talking shit about why he wanted me to rescue the ambassador and how much she would be missed. He told me nothing about the where and why." She *had* expected more; people were going on a rescue mission using his sub-par information, and that wasn't good enough. "It was his assistant who gave me a briefing of sorts. Apparently, your guys had been heavy-handed in their suggestion they lead the op, so Lawrence decided that our help would be minimal. His assistant couldn't give me much information except the details of our assets, but he hoped that I'd get a confidential report before we left." Mitch shook her head. "His ego is bruised, and he doesn't like that the Brits have an agency dedicated to helping women. Asshole."

Alex nodded slowly. "That explains so much. Thank you for sharing it with me."

"I'll do a good job. I'll back you up, for sure. My old boss wants to promote me, and I need this chance to show I can do it." Mitch tracked a group of guys who she thought were standing too close to a couple of women at the bar, but their body language suggested they were comfortable enough. She looked back at Alex. "I need to show more forethought. I nearly always get results, but there are often casualties and a little too much noise. I take risks to get shit done, and the higher-ups don't always appreciate that. I'm working on how to slow myself down, but slowing down can sometimes mean the difference between life and death."

Alex bit her lip. "It's a difficult line to straddle in our work. The risks are the important thing to consider in an op, and where those risks can be taken and where they should be avoided. Sometimes the old adage 'slowly, slowly, catchy monkey' is what's needed."

"That's a very weird saying. I don't know if I can do that." Mitch glanced at Alex, and she raised her eyebrows, her expression grim. "I'm being honest. It may not be what you want to hear, but I'm saying that I'll try. I'm not one to sit around and talk things to death if jumping in is what's best."

"As the leader of this operation, I'll do my best to listen to you, but I need to keep you on a short leash. I intend to consider all aspects before we head off into an armed conflict. I don't want any casualties.' She rubbed her face and looked tired. "I'll usually spend days getting to know my team. It helps to understand them as people and not just as words on a background briefing."

"And here you are, stuck with me and a load of mercenaries. That's a whole lot of leashes you need to keep in hand. Although there could be other uses for that leash." Mitch wiggled her eyebrows and grinned.

Alex chuckled and shook her head. "As you may have gathered, I like to make sure I have as much information as possible before I make a decision. Maps, obviously, but intel reports, political reports, and any interviews or whatever else I can get my hands on. I joined the army straight from school and ended up in the Special Intelligence Service, getting experience in intelligence gathering and then I went on to black ops." She hesitated. "Mitch, I'm not saying your way of doing things is wrong, or that I won't consider other options, but I do believe in the power of words and intelligence over acts of aggression."

There wasn't any point in arguing whose approach was better. Mitch was all about reacting to the situation as needed, whichever way that led. "With what little extra my guys have added, do we have enough information?" They probably had *too* much, which would muddy the waters when it came to operations on the ground. Her initial thoughts about the slow processes the Brits employed clearly weren't wrong.

"We have to take what we have, and get on with it," Alex said.

Mitch was being placated, but she let it go. Hell, maybe she'd learn a thing or two about leadership and overthinking from Alex, things she could use to get that damn promotion.

"As far as running an op, think about what our bosses are looking for and what they need briefing on and who we need to talk to first. We need to show them we're doing what's expected. Diplomacy first. Understand? Keep the bosses and clients happy first off. You'll have both the Embassy and the White House to keep in the loop."

"Mm. That's something I've never considered. I just *do*." *Fuck knuckles*. She hadn't considered all the liaising she was going to have to do in addition to finding the ambassador.

"And in between talking to the High Commission and the government, we take time out and talk to your guys about an armed retrieval and see if they can locate the ambassador. That way, we're covering both angles."

"What you're saying is that we're going to waste a lot of time talking instead of covering actual ground," Mitch said, rubbing her forehead. "And that's why I think we should split up when we get there. Then my guys can be on the move, gathering information while you're talking to people too high up to even see the ground."

Alex blanched. "We have very different approaches, I think."

"I suppose we should leave now." Mitch tapped her watch. "We have an early morning. I'd be happy to join you for the night." She grinned. "We're not technically on the op yet. We could blow off some steam, get rid of pre-launch nerves."

"I can see what you're doing, Lieutenant Brennan, and no." Alex's smile reached her eyes. "We're sleeping in our own beds tonight. I can't afford to take my focus from the op for even a moment."

"I'll walk you home," Mitch said.

"There's no need," Alex said. "I'm not some fragile woman who needs handholding."

"I get that, but I want a little more time with you, and this is a good opportunity."

Alex slid on her jacket. "Okay, you can walk me home, but

you're not coming in. Understand?"

Mitch watched the gentle sway of Alex's hips as they left the restaurant. Opposites could attract, sure, but when one was the boss, it made things messy. Mitch had avoided that as she'd climbed the ladder, determined never to let a woman distract her. But as they stepped into the cool night air, and Alex's breath clouded between them, she had a feeling she'd never really known what messy could be.

CHAPTER NINE

As the plane began its descent, Alex pressed her nose to the glass and looked out the window at the African landscape. She hadn't spent any time in Minabo during her work in Africa, but the landscape below could have been any of a dozen African countries she knew well: the same heat and the savannah, hills and the trees, jungle in the reaches of the mountains and rain that helped and hindered life. Water fell by the bucket load, and she shuddered at the thought of the African floods that had swept people, animals, and homes away leaving those areas devastated. She hoped that didn't happen while they were there.

"You seemed excited when we set off, but now you look strangely sad," Mitch said.

"I was thinking about the floods and the devastation they cause. Somehow, when you're away from somewhere and look back to the past, the sun is always shining. I'd forgotten the bad stuff."

Mitch nodded. "I get that." Then she pointed through the window. "Look, there's a herd of animals over there. Giraffes? Yup. Goddamn giraffes. Wow. Never seen anything like that before."

"We may get to see them close up before we finish," Alex said. "I love giraffes. They're my favorite."

"Remind me I might need a gun and some ammo when we go out," Mitch said and laughed.

Alex swallowed hard at the subtle fragrance of Mitch's cologne and got up the moment the seat belt sign blinked out. She left the plane and was hit by the hot African air, which smelled just as she remembered. Yes, there was the smell of avgas, but there was something else too. It was difficult to quantify, but the air was full of earth, and sun, and sky, and the clean scent of Africa. She walked quickly through the airport with Mitch following along behind, and she slowed down to save Mitch from almost running. She hadn't really realized that she took such long steps until the night before when, even strolling along, she was leaving Mitch behind. It mattered to her that they walked together. Mitch hadn't commented, but she guessed that Mitch liked to take the lead in some things, and her racing ahead all the time put Mitch firmly in the back seat.

They entered the arrivals area, and she saw a man holding a cardboard sign with BENNET written in a Sharpie. He was in the usual gear of chauffeurs the world over with white shirt, black trousers, and black shoes. "I'm Bennet," she said.

"Hello, madam. We're going to visit the giraffes; is that correct?" He spoke perfect English, but his emphasis was overly posh.

"Perfect," Alex said. "And who are you?"

"Thomas, madam. Let me take you to our vehicle."

Alex smiled at his pronunciation. "Lead on, Thomas. We're happy to see some of your beautiful country."

Thomas took her suitcase and headed toward the door.

"I see why I need to get promoted now. So I have someone to carry my cases to the ve-Hicle." Mitch laughed as she carried her own case behind them.

Thomas took them to a gray saloon car with no markings. He set off quickly, heading into Solunwa. Along the road, there were some new and modern buildings juxtaposed with old, rickety structures in a poor state of repair. There was a walkway of sorts on either side of the road, crowded with people moving in both directions. It looked as if they'd left a football stadium, but here, it was the usual daily foot traffic.

Alex had seen a lot of cities in Africa, but Solunwa took her breath away. It was the traffic that defied all description. There were white minivans everywhere, often six deep on the road and all going in different directions. Each van was crammed full of people, and they seemed to stop randomly and without notice. At the top of a slight hill, the vision below them was of a never-ending flow of white vehicles between mostly single-story buildings. The air smelled of stale sewage, warm vegetables, and oily smoke.

Thomas closed the windows and switched on the A/C. "I'm sorry, the air conditioning is not efficient in most of our High Commission cars, but the fragrance of the air is not good until we get further through the city."

"There's so much traffic," Alex said, trying not to breathe in the warm, recycled air "I don't recall that it was so heavy in my time in other parts of Africa."

"We are expanding as a country, and we have more businesses and more workers who all need to travel to and from work." He accelerated around a motorcycle with several boxes of chickens on the back.

"Have the government considered a railway?" Mitch asked. "That would remove most of the traffic, wouldn't it?"

"Yes, madam. I believe the government have been looking for the money from foreign investment for this already." He turned to look at them whilst still driving at some considerable speec. "I think the Chinese have decided to help us out with that. There is talk that they will have much investment here." He turned back anc sighed. "I think the Great British High Commission will have to leave the country, the same as the United States of America."

"That must be difficult for you," Alex said.

"Yes, madam. Her Excellency has said she will help me all she can if she has to leave. I am hoping that I can get another job as a personal chauffeur, but the competition is stiff."

Mitch made a non-committal sound of agreement, though she didn't look up from her phone, where her thumbs moved at speed as she sent multiple texts. Alex sighed. So much for being diplomatic. She couldn't even talk nicely to their driver.

Thomas drove them to the High Commission gates, and one of the guards there stopped them for ID from Alex and Mitch before waving them through. Alex placed her hand over her heart as it threatened to beat out of her chest. The op was finally starting, and whatever happened from this moment on was going to be important. Thomas took them through a couple of courtyards and stopped outside a building that looked no different to any of the others around the High Commission grounds.

He turned around. "There are guest quarters here, and I've been asked to drop you at the door. Reception inside will show you your rooms," he said and got out of the car. He opened the trunk and removed their luggage quickly. "The high commissioner will see you as soon as you are settled. Please go through the building opposite and follow the signs. She will be free from four thirty."

"Thank you, Thomas. You've been both welcoming and helpful," Alex said.

Mitch gave him a quick nod as she picked up both their cases and headed inside.

Alex followed Mitch into the building, and they were directed to their rooms. She opened the door to her room, then stopped as Mitch entered the room opposite. "Do you have something with you that's suitable to wear to meet the high commissioner?" Alex looked Mitch up and down, and though she very much admired the way her belted, low-slung black jeans and black T-shirt with black leather motorcycle boots suited her body and personality perfectly, it wasn't suitable for a more formal meeting with the British Ambassador.

"You mean this isn't good enough?" Mitch grinned. "Do you want to come in and dress me yourself?"

"No, thank you. I'll knock on your door at four twenty," Alex said and closed the door. She leaned against it, listening for the sound of Mitch's door. It seemed to take longer than it should... When it finally closed, Alex took a breath. Separate rooms was good, but it might have been better if they were in different wings of the building altogether. How was she supposed to sleep with Mitch right across the hall?

The room was a reasonable size. It was "embassy-plain," with white walls, gray carpet, and no decorations. That was perfect. No distractions of any kind. She quickly emptied her case and placed everything in the right space. She took her toiletries into the bathroom, quickly stripped off, and was in the shower within moments. The water had a unique smell, as foreign water often did, but it was still warm and refreshing.

She dressed in a light-weight beige pantsuit with a pale pink silk sleeveless top underneath. Sandals completed the outfit, then she added some light makeup and a spray of perfume. Ready early, she took the opportunity to sit on her bed underneath the antiquated air-conditioning system to get her thoughts in order so that she could brief the high commissioner, Beth Tregawn. She opened her leather binder and read over her notes.

She hadn't met Tregawn, but she'd known of her in her days in Africa. Tregawn was a career diplomat and had been especially effective in helping deal with the Ebola outbreak in Sierra Leone. Alex hoped that Her Excellency would ensure that the British response to the kidnapping would be fast and straightforward. She laughed. Nothing in Africa was *ever* fast or straightforward, and they were already having to deal with an awkward relationship with the US.

She knocked on Mitch's door, and it was thrown open before she'd finished knocking. Mitch had gelled her hair and was wearing black pants, a black fitted shirt with a dark gray vest, and a black and gray striped tie. Her boots were black leather and looked expensive. Alex couldn't take her eyes off her. She looked her up and down again, before finally tearing her gaze away.

Mitch jutted her chin. "Like what you see?

"Yes, you look...good," Alex said, the heat rising in her face as she took in the way Mitch's clothes hugged her muscular form.

Mitch smirked and leaned against the doorframe. "Just good, huh?"

Alex turned away. *Busted.* It was no good saying one thing and doing another. She was sending mixed messages; the surreptitious stares and outright ogling had to stop. But that was easier said than done. "Are you happy with what we discussed on the plane? I'll take the lead in the briefing, and then you can talk about the US contribution."

"Works for me. And we call her 'your excellency' unless she says otherwise. Got it." Mitch rolled her eyes a little. "I've messaged the asset leader to let him know we've arrived and that we'll meet him as soon as we can."

"Excellent," Alex said.

They arrived at the ante room, and a young woman looked up as they arrived. "Hello, I'm Ann, the commissioner's assistant. I'm to show you straight in. Would you like tea, coffee, or a soft drink?"

"Tea," said Alex. "Milk, no sugar."

"Coffee." Mitch smiled at Ann. "Strong and black, please."

Alex couldn't help but be jealous of Mitch's flirtatious smile, and the way Ann smiled back suggested she appreciated the undertone. *Focus.* Beth Tregawn was both highly intelligent and a well-respected career diplomat, and they needed her detailed knowledge of the government and her negotiating ability if they were to succeed. She couldn't be pouting about a woman she wasn't even involved with.

Following introductions, Beth offered them seats.

"I don't know how up to date you are, Your Excellency, but might I brief you on the operation as we see it? Then perhaps you can share any information you may have."

"Perfect," Beth said.

"We would like to try to end this whole kidnapping issue diplomatically, as I'm sure you do. However, it would appear that the US, having been removed from the country, has not been allowed any say in the ambassador's rescue." She took a sip of tea. "If we can't negotiate a diplomatic solution with whomever has taken the ambassador, or a solution involving the Minabo armed forces, we'll have to take action ourselves. To do this, we'll use American assets who have stayed in Minabo as civilians following deployment for their country a few years ago." Alex nodded toward Mitch. "Hence the joint team of myself and Lieutenant Brennan."

"If we get word from our contacts as to the whereabouts of the ambassador," Mitch said, "and there's no other option, we'll aim to rescue her ourselves using as little violence as possible. We've come up with a number of possible ways to find her. We're certain her captors will be armed and have planned accordingly."

"How many assets will you call on?" Beth asked. Her expression gave nothing away, even though she was asking about armed expats in motion on African soil.

"I expect to have two teams of ten," Mitch said. "Some are resident in Minabo and some in surrounding countries. They're making their way here."

"We've managed to source what arms we need," Alex said, nodding again at Mitch, "but we'll keep it undercover, so whatever happens—if you need it—you'll have deniability."

"That's good to know," Beth said. "I'm hoping that the president will see you and agree to use his forces to sort this whole mess out. But I'm not hopeful. I had thought that he would want this resolved quickly and quietly, but I was wrong. When I spoke to him, he considered the ambassador foolish and wasn't concerned about her. He seemed certain she'd simply turn up."

Alex frowned. That seemed strange. "Before we left the UK, we hadn't received any ransom demands, so we're unsure as to why the ambassador was taken or where she's likely to be. We're hopeful she is still in Minabo and hasn't been taken over the border into South Sudan."

Beth nodded, her expression turning sour. "I managed to see the president yesterday, and he has no update on the ambassador's whereabouts. I'll be frank. He doesn't appear to have done anything to get that information either. To my face, he's apologetic that it's happened and is concerned for his tourist industry, but in truth, he thinks she was silly to have come to Minabo in the first place, especially alone." Her face turned red, and she slapped the desk. "There are no restrictions on any tourists, so why shouldn't she come? I said as much to the president, and he just smiled. I could almost hear him say, 'and here's another silly woman.' Men." She wrinkled her nose. "So any information we gather will have to be without the aid of the government. I've quietly attempted to find information using my own resources, but so far..." She gave an elegant shrug. "It's like she simply vanished."

That was about the worst news they could have gotten. "Do you think the president will see us?" Alex asked.

"Yes, I think he has to. I've asked his office for an appointment for you. You're a joint US/UK deputation, and he can't simply ignore you. But I suspect you'll be kept waiting as a show of his power and strength. And don't expect much in the way of honest respect. But he'll see you eventually, so that he can tell our countries that he has assisted us. That means Minabo will get more of our relief money. I hope you have better luck with him than I did. You should be aware, though, that he won't be happy to have an American in your entourage, and I don't suggest you tell him you're employing mercenaries." She stood, indicating their meeting was coming to an end.

"Is there anyone else we can approach on outside channels who might help?" Alex asked.

"There's an ex-minister who may be able to help you, but I'm not sure how. He's the tribal chief of the Dorobo, but he has little power and may not have any useful information. I've asked him to speak with you, and my assistant will set you up with an appointment. In the meantime, let her know what's happening. She'll put you through if you need me."

Alex and Mitch followed the commissioner to the door. "Thank you for your time, Your Excellency," Alex said.

"Good luck," Beth said and shook their hands.

How much of that luck were they going to need?

* * *

Alex didn't know how long her patience would last. Working the last couple of years in the UK had meant that she'd forgotten the way life in Africa meandered like a parched river moving across the plain to the coast. She and Mitch managed to get an audience with Mathenge Mizumbo, the senior tribal chief of the Dorobo. He lived in a large brick-built house not far from the Commission. With imposing gates and a long driveway surrounded by lush gardens, it was difficult to think of the relative poverty outside the gates.

Mizumbo, a short, rather rotund man, greeted them personally and invited them in for tea.

"Thank you. I'm happy with tea." Alex saw Mitch stiffen. "But my colleague, Ms. Brennan, is a coffee drinker. If you don't have coffee, water will be fine."

"Of course. Pearl will look after us all." He gestured toward a woman who appeared after they'd entered the house. She nodded and left the hall.

Mizumbo indicated they should follow him into a library with bookshelves filled floor-to-ceiling on every wall. They sat in deep red leather armchairs, and Alex started a conversation about the different books Mizumbo had, discovering he was interested in British historical stories about people such as Captain Hornblower in the Royal Navy and Sharpe who was in the British Army in Europe and had fought Napolean Bonaparte. Mitch practically vibrated with obvious frustration at the unnecessary small talk, but building relationships took time.

Pearl entered with drinks and a slice of Victoria sponge for each of them.

"You can see why I'm not as slim as I might be." He patted his stomach and laughed deeply. "I understand you're looking for the American Ambassador," he said.

"Yes, sir," Alex said. "We've had no information and wonder if you had contacts that could perhaps help us? The British High Commissioner suggested that you were friendly toward our countries, and I would hope they may be able to help you in return."

She looked across at Mitch, who nodded. Mitch may have said she didn't do strategy, but she obviously understood what was required.

"Exactly so. Madam Commissioner has been very helpful to me over the last months, and I am hopeful that we can continue our relationship." He took a mouthful of cake. "The only information I have is that the ambassador may have been taken north. That part of the country is mostly grasslands until the border with southern Sudan. It is difficult to communicate, and the phone signal is poor. But I'm hopeful I will get word if anyone knows where she is. I'm sorry I have nothing more useful at this time."

They finished their conversation, talking about the places to visit in Minabo before Mizumbo ushered them to their car. He promised to contact the commissioner if he had any news.

"I'm glad I don't have to do that as a damn job." Mitch snorted as they left the grounds. "I mean, the coffee and cake were delicious, but all the polite smiling and making conversation were way out of my comfort zone. It's all so...boring."

"I know what you mean, especially when we got no immediate results," Alex said. "But when he gives us some good information, you'll be saying how simple it was to have a *boring* conversation and get real intel."

Two days later, they were still waiting for the call to see the president and had no new information.

Despite Mitch wanting to see her contacts without Alex, she stuck around, for which Alex was grateful, even though it was like watching a caged lion, pacing and looking for a way out of confinement. If Mitch had been out actually doing things while Alex was stuck waiting, it would have been much worse. What trouble could Mitch and her fellow gung-ho soldiers get into without Alex there to oversee them? She shuddered at the possibilities.

Alex agreed to meet with Mitch's contacts as soon as the appointment with the president had happened. They'd looked at possible scenarios and liaised with the other agencies involved, all of whom were none too pleased with the lack of information. There was little else to do until they had met the president to discuss using Minabo's military or to discover other information about where the ambassador was.

On the third morning, Alex ate breakfast at the small table they'd been using, but Mitch didn't show. She knocked on her door, but there was no answer. Several texts went unanswered. By the time lunch came around, Alex's head ached from her bad temper, and she was most definitely going to give Mitch a piece of her mind when she finally showed up.

Her phone pinged and she grabbed it. *The president will see you in one hour.* Well, that was something. But damn it all, where was Mitch? She sent a message letting Mitch know the appointment time and then got ready, making sure she looked every inch the responsible operative.

Alex stood outside the president's building, which, in terms of the architecture in the country, could be termed a palace. It was a grand structure with columns and arches, and she assumed it contained the government of Minabo and all their offices. But Mizumbo had explained this was the president's home and office, and four wives lived there with him. Alex looked up the marble steps that seemed to rise forever. They were obviously to reinforce the difference in ranking between visitors and the man who ruled the country. It was a tactic used by men whose power was more fragile than they wanted it to be.

So this was going to be one of *those* meetings. The fact that Mitch was missing was enough to make her sick. She'd probably decided to meet her assets alone. And that meant she'd left Alex to deal with this herself. *For the best, probably. Who knows what kind of thing she'd say?*

She put her foot on the bottom step and looked up to the top of the stairway to see the president standing at the top waiting for her. He wore a military dress uniform with a chest full of medals and a couple of larger star insignia. Yep, just as she thought: a power-hungry man making a point. She didn't look up again and kicked herself for looking up at all.

"Madame Hartley, I assume. Welcome to our magnificent country," he said.

Alex nodded. "Good afternoon, Mr. President."

"Come into my office, and we shall discuss the missing ambassador."

Alex followed him into the building. Sculptures and African artefacts cluttered the corridor, windows were covered by louvred shutters, and woven brocade gold-colored curtains hung almost superfluously at the sides.

His office was dark mahogany and leather with the same louvred windows, and brocade curtains highlighted a repeat pattern of a tribal shield and spears.

"You have a beautiful office, sir," Alex said. And how much foreign money had he used to build it?

"I am lucky; I have been able to use my fortune to upgrade the buildings to suit me. My wives are grateful too, as it means that my many children are able to live well and receive a good education. In the future, they could become our country's rulers."

"Have you had any news about the American ambassador?" Alex didn't want to hear about his enormous eighteen-child family and how much better off they were than the people he was supposed to be serving. Her diving straight in to what she needed to know wasn't very politic, but he didn't seem put off by it.

"Nothing as yet, but I am not worried. This is a large country, and there are many places that she could have wandered off to. I have people looking for her, and I am sure that word will come soon enough."

"I hope so," Alex said. "It would be a shame to think that your tourist industry might suffer if the word spreads worldwide that your country is dangerous."

He waved like he was shooing away a fly. "That won't happen.

The country is colorful and vibrant, with exotic wildlife that they want to see. A little trouble now and then will not put people off. We are a peaceful country. Only a handful of our people are ungrateful and want more. We will be quick to resolve the situation once the ambassador is found."

"I'm pleased that you agree that we need to find the ambassador quickly, though I'm not sure that an ambassador being kidnapped counts as 'a little trouble.'" She smiled, and his eyes hardened. "And both the United States of America and His Majesty's government in Great Britain look forward to getting the ambassador back safely and quickly.'

"Perhaps after the Americans were asked to leave, their ambassador should not have come here for her holidays." His smile didn't soften his gaze. "Though of course, she was welcome as a tourist, as anyone would be. I am sure she will be found soon in the company of some villager or other who has offered to show her the best of life here." He sat behind the enormous desk. "It has been a pleasure, madame. Nitusi will show you out." He held up his hand before she got to the door. "I trust you will inform me of any information you may receive, so that we can handle things correctly. We wouldn't want any further misunderstandings."

Alex had no option but to leave. The president hadn't offered or allowed her to ask for extra assistance, and his position was clear. Suggesting the ambassador was simply off enjoying herself didn't take into account the witness statements or the dead driver. Was he trying to paint a picture where nothing had gone wrong, and their governments had simply over-reacted?

So the effort to retrieve the ambassador was down to her and Mitch, if she could ever bring Mitch to heel so they didn't cause an international incident or scandal. But...now that they had no government assistance, was it time to let Mitch take the lead? *God help us.*

CHAPTER TEN

MITCH MANEUVERED THE BORROWED BM150 motorbike on a street teeming with traffic. But even with the noise, pollution, and traffic, it was damn good to be out of that government waiting room. She felt a little bad about not letting Alex know her plans, but she just couldn't sit around any longer, and Alex wasn't about to break away from her precious rulebook to get things moving. And being so close to her every day, only being able to look and not touch, didn't make it easy to ignore the growing attraction that had no place on the plains of Africa.

Mitch had gotten directions from her assets and headed out to the south of Solunwa about thirty minutes away by bike. She came to a number of roadside stores, which were nothing more than sheds, with items piled high on the ground. Mitch had been instructed to turn left at the store selling soap.

She followed the directions and turned until she came to a long corrugated metal shed with *bike repairs and sales* scrawled in large white letters along the side. *And trucks and cars* had been added under the word bike. She came to a stop at the open end of the building in front of a group of mostly white men, dressed for the weather and looking every inch like the ex-military they were.

One of the men came forward and held out his hand. "Ma'am, pleased to meet ya," he said. "I'm Green."

"Mitch." She got off her bike and shook his hand.

"Half these men are the Green Team, and work with me. The other half is the Blue Team, working with an Australian-American we call Blue. In Aussie slang, blue means red. Jim Redd e is called Blue because of his last name, so his team are the Blue Team." He grinned. "Complicated, eh?"

"Not really." Mitch laughed. "Let's have a look at what you have here, and what you're going to need."

She followed Green into the back of the building, and he opened a door into a small room. "We've got actual bike parts in here for show. We've told the locals that we'll shoot anyone trying to get at our gear."

"Where's your store?" Mitch asked, expecting to see evidence of their weapons and vehicles.

"That what's so good about this place. Our entrance is here."

He moved a large wooden crate labelled *forks* and beneath it was a metal sheet. He knocked three times, and the trapdoor lifted. Mitch followed Green down a ladder into a basement.

"This is what's good about our security. You don't get down here unless we're expecting you. Smile for the camera," he said, pointing and looking into the corner of the small underground cavern.

Mitch followed suit. They walked along an underground tunnel for about a quarter of a mile before coming out into an enormous cavern that stretched as far as Mitch could see.

"Where the fuck are we?" Mitch tried not to show her surprise as she stared at a variety of heavy machinery that had no business being underground.

"This is a played-out gold mine. The locals think we're looking for gold, and we let them think it. We fix bikes at the front and use this area to bring down whatever we need. We could blow a small hole in the town with all this," Green said.

"Gold mining? That's a great cover."

"Yep, occasionally we come up with something small, take it to town and trade it for a few beers."

"Have you had any hits for the ambassador yet?" Mitch asked.

"No, but someone's calling in tonight, so I'll let you know. We've got scouts searching local villages and asking questions. Someone somewhere will know something." Green jutted his chin. "So, we've got an English toff in charge, do we? She okay?"

"Yeah, she's fine. I'll bring her out eventually. But I'm your boss, and if you want to get paid, you do what I need you to when I need you to."

"I get that," Green said. "It's a US op to get back a US official, but you're letting the Brit think she's in charge."

"Yeah, pretty much," Mitch said, though Alex would be pissed that Mitch had gone AWOL when she got back.

"Where d'ya work normally, if you can say?" Green asked.

"Texas border," Mitch said.

Green nodded, as though he'd been around that block. "Did think about going back for some of that, but the life here is good, and we get enough work to keep us out of trouble. Nice women too." He smiled and winked.

Mitch couldn't comment; they hadn't exactly been sightseeing. "Once we know where the ambassador is being held, we go in, armed with enough to deal with the natives but holding back on the heavy guns. That good with you?"

Green nodded. "Got it. Around here, we go in light until we have to go in heavy. No sense in raising lots of red flags. My only concern is how far we've got to travel for the retrieval. I reckon she's in the north somewhere, out where the most disenfranchised are, and most of that is hard to reach. It's gonna be a hike to get there, and that'll delay us. Still no ransom note?"

Mitch shook her head. "Do we have access to light aircraft? We'd need enough room for your two teams plus me and the Brit. Do you have contacts?"

"Blue'll handle that." Green tilted his head slightly. "It won't be cheap, but they can get us as close as they can."

"Thanks. I need to get back to the capital. Let me know when your scouts report back tonight, and I'll leave whatever swanky party I'm being my best self at," Mitch said.

Green laughed. "I'm sure they love you up there. American woman who could take them out? Just their type."

Mitch chuckled; he wasn't wrong. But she was more concerned about what she should tell Alex and when, and she'd have to apologize for going off the reservation without "permission." But time was ticking, and it wasn't up to Alex. This was US business to rescue the US ambassador, and they were US contractors risking their lives. She was in charge of this team, and she had to make sure she could count on them. Green was just the sort of guy she'd expected to find, more than equipped to give her what she needed.

She could handle mercs, she could handle kidnappings, and she could handle cartels. Why, then, was she concerned about facing Alex's wrath when she got back?

CHAPTER ELEVEN

Jessica's feet hurt like she'd been walking barefoot on pebbles. Her chest ached and her thighs burned. They walked across what felt like the entirety of the Minabo savannah. There was some similarity with the American prairie, although there were more trees here. The chief led the way, sure-footed and acting as a guide, like this was a tourist excursion and not a kidnapping. The pace was steady, but she was still having to push herself to keep up. The sweat ran from her body in rivulets, with dust joining the sweat to create a layer of grit. When she set off, she had wiped the sweat off with the cloth Lulu had given her. But all too soon, she wasn't bothering with it and just continued the interminable walking.

Mukasa handed her a bottle of water. "Use this sparingly as we cannot fill it up until we get to Baku, and we only have what we are carrying. The villages you are going to visit have no water pipes and store only what they can carry in plastic containers from the nearest water point."

"So how many days until we get fresh water?" Jessica asked, eyeing the bottle that she would normally have gulped down in minutes.

"I am taking you to only some of the villages here, just four of the hundreds. But I want you to see where your aid money should be going, and how these people are having to live without it," Mukasa said. "You need to see to understand. It's the only way."

Joseph moved closer as they walked. "Many people think we should make an example of you. They want to kill you to make a big country like America see we have power. If you die, they'll send top men from your country, and they will see that their money is missing."

She quelled her irritation as he talked almost conversationally, like he wasn't talking about murdering her. "That's what *you* think. But I can talk to the people who handle the money, and you need to show me what's going on, just like your father says. Let me see what's wrong, and I'll see what I can do to change things." She kept her voice steady, focusing on the pain in her feet instead of on the fear rippling through her.

"Yes, but that's all talk." He shook his head, his jaw clenched. "You will say whatever is needed to get you out of this. But if you are dead, the message is made, and we are a step further along the way."

Mukasa came over and took Joseph's arm. "Stop. You have agreed we will do this my way, and the villages have all agreed too. Jessica will see how we have to live, even though their money is supposed to be helping us."

Joseph and his friends, who had left Jessica alone for most of the day, looked her up and down and started jeering again. The chief spoke sharply, and silence followed.

The sun was low in the sky, indicating the end of the day, when Jessica made out the silhouettes of some huts on the horizon ahead. Having looked at an almost endlessly flat horizon, the village was a welcome sight. She could sit and allow her shaking legs to recover. Her feet were blistered, bloody, and stuck to the borrowed sandals, making her limp. She hadn't begged to stop today, but if she had to do this walk again tomorrow, it might become necessary.

A whole host of villagers came out to see their party arrive, and they stared hard at Jessica as she limped past. The village didn't appear to be anywhere near as tidy as the chief's. The children were too thin, and the adults were gaunt and haunted looking. The huts were broken down, and the cattle and goats were nearly shadows.

She tried to straighten herself up and be the ambassador, but she had little left after the day's trek. She was dirty and unkempt, wearing borrowed clothes and walking like an old woman. An elderly man leaning on a walking stick came across and greeted Mukasa.

"This is the chief of this village, Chief Hanaku," Mukasa said, "and he bids you welcome. We will sit and eat, and afterward, you will take care of your personal needs before sleep. Tomorrow, we will have a discussion with the chief and the villagers from here and the surrounding villages. We will then head to the next village."

The news that they'd be walking the next morning nearly made her weep, but she just nodded and followed them to an open fire pit. She gingerly lowered herself onto a mat and was grateful when a young woman took her arm to help her down. She made a noise of sympathy when she looked at Jessica's feet, then walked away.

As the villagers prepared a meal in communal style, an air of excitement built. Were they truly glad she was there? She worried that they were expecting a lot of her, and she didn't know whether or not she could deliver. She thought back to the days when she was young and working in different political offices, gaining experience and thinking about changing the world. She'd gone into politics knowing that those with political influence could affect the allocation of resources, and it could ensure their power. When had she stopped caring about how things were done? When had she stopped paying attention, allowing others to determine the rules of the game? She'd helped put a president in place yet now she was nothing but one pawn of many, and all her hopes and dreams from the past had somehow slipped away.

A woman sat beside her, holding a small infant who didn't cry or fuss. She simply lay in her mother's arms, staring at nothing. Jessica swallowed hard and gently touched the child's head. Maybe she *could* do something that would help these people. *If* she lived through this. *If* she made it home.

The meal was served by the women, and Jessica was allowed to remain seated with the men and some of the more senior women. She ate the food presented to her, though she barely tasted it. Ravenous and exhausted, she would have eaten just about anything. When she finished, she let the firelight lull her into a doze and was awakened by Mukasa, who handed her a cup of beer.

"This is not strong and will be good to ensure you have enough liquid. I have a water bottle for you here as well," he said. "One of the women will take you to the facilities and show you to where you will sleep. Good night. I will see you tomorrow."

"Thank you," she said, then she hobbled behind a woman, who said she was called Star, to a hole in the ground that was so fetid, she gagged. There was no water for washing and no shower as far as she could see. Once again, she was provided with a mat to sleep on alongside the women and children. Jessica used the mosquite net Lulu had given her and was glad of it, though no one else had one. Guilt tore through her for having something even the children didn't have, an absence that put their lives at risk. But exhaustion overtook her, and she fell into a deep, dreamless sleep.

The following morning, she was awakened gently by Star, who showed her to an area where there were some bowls for personal washing. She took water from one of the large containers, and Star showed her the art of using only a little water and the same leaves she'd used before to clean herself up. Star gently helped her wash the blisters on her feet, and though Jessica hissed a little at the pain, it was good when they were free of grit. The cheap canvas shoes had probably saved her from getting any serious infection. Star showed her a round scar on one of the children's feet from a burrowing worm, which infected feet from the land being used as a public toilet. Once again, she gagged and had to take a sip of water.

Millions. Millions of dollars in aid have been sent here. Where the hell had it gone? Had it just been used in the cities? How corrupt had things become?

After she'd had some breakfast and Mukasa had translated for the village chief as he told her about the problems they faced daily, they were on their way to yet another village and a long day's walk on sore feet. The village of Nanakama looked even more poverty-stricken than Baku, and the villagers greeted them when they arrived. Their chief showed them around. There were huts in ruins and some needed repair. The children were mostly naked and moved around quietly. One of the chief's sons had a truck so rusted that it looked like it had been stolen from a junkyard. He helped them get water, and although it was a long and bumpy journey, it saved them more arduous walking.

"This isn't the poorest village out here, but you can see how distance from the charities means they get minimal help or no help at all," Mukasa said.

Jessica nodded. There was little that needed to be said about the poverty and lack of the basics like water and toilet facilities.

Mukasa helped her climb in the back of the truck without having to open the door, since it was missing, and several of the villagers who wanted to visit friends and family in the next village joined them. The chief's son started the truck, and it sounded like a wounded lion. Jessica endured the worst journey by transport she'd ever had. The truck had no suspension, and it jarred her in every direction like she was in a tumble dryer. Her whole body ached, and muscles spasmed as she tried to keep herself from being tossed from side to side on the tracks, which were little more than paths animals had created. No one else seemed overly concerned, and several laughed at her when she bounced particularly high after hitting a deep rut.

Two hours later, she managed to get down from the vehicle without much assistance, and she was pleased to see another village that had a number of separate settlements within it. It appeared well cared for, and Jessica could see some of their cattle out on the grasslands beyond the village. She lingered by the truck to watch the proceedings, happy just to be alone for a few moments. She'd been surrounded by people ever since she'd been kidnapped, and while she usually feared being alone, she tried not to think of that today. But it was no good. She was lost, exhausted, and wanted to go home. She eventually followed along behind everyone else before someone sent Joseph or his men to fetch her.

There were a lot of villagers, and visitors as well, dressed in different colored clothing, and there were greetings going back and forth. As the afternoon progressed it became obvious there was going to be a big meeting. Mukasa made sure Jessica had plenty of water, and she sat undisturbed in the center of the village for some time, watching and thinking, and glad to be sitting in the shade.

Joseph was surrounded by a group of young men who seemed to respect him. He talked and they listened, and more than one shot looks her way. Fear, her constant companion of the last several days, made her cold even in the heat of the day. She looked away and focused on the group gathering under the awning. Men formed a kind of inner ring, with women and children spread out beyond them. Many stared at her, and she could only hope they weren't of Joseph's mindset. It was the last village they had to visit. Maybe they'd let her go home after this.

Mukasa stood at the front and thanked Chief Mutesi for allowing everyone into his village. He motioned for Jessica to join him in the clearing and introduced her. She couldn't imagine what she must look like. But they didn't care, did they? They didn't care about her wrinkled clothes or matted hair. They needed food and water, not someone in Gucci telling them things would be fine.

He spoke in mostly his own language, then repeated everything in English. "We have a lot to talk about, and I know you all want to tell the ambassador the problems with water, and sanitation, and cooking, about the children and their health and education." He looked at Jessica. "Ambassador, you have seen how we live in the bush, the grasslands of northern Minabo and the lands of the Kakuku. We have lived here since our forefathers first roamed the land. Our bodies and souls sink back into the earth once we are no more," he said to nods from a number of the men and some words that seemed to be in agreement. "Now our lands are being stolen. Firstly, a farmer is offered some small money for the property and land. This is more than he has seen in his lifetime, and he becomes greedy and says yes, I'll take it. The ambassador knows about this."

"Is there anyone here that this had happened to?" Jessica asked. Two men put up their hands. "Will you speak to me afterward?"

One of the men nodded. The other looked at him, and he translated, and then he also nodded.

"The other way the land is stolen is that the government says to people like me, with several hundred head of cattle out grazing, that I have to show the land that is mine by fencing it, and if I do not, they will seize the land. But I have no money to buy the fencing, and if I did fence some, my cattle would not have enough room to graze anyway. I would lose my livelihood."

Someone shouted from the back, and Mukasa waved him off.

"I'm getting there, Daniko," he said. "We all know that the people making these demands are our chiefs in government who receive the grants that the American and British Governments are sending as aid to help our country. Madam Ambassador, to explain, the chiefs in the government are the most senior of our chiefs. There are then chiefs in charge of local government. They report to the senior chiefs. And then there are chiefs like me, who run our own villages. I am different because I have an honorary position as a chief in charge of villages on the savannah. I get no money, no votes for anything. But I try to look out for the villages. In the past, our government chiefs ensured that money was given to everyone, so they were seen to be fair. Now it is all about grabbing as much as they can, and the poorest, like us, have no chance."

The gathered villagers continued to nod and agree.

"Madam Ambassador, we brought you here so you could see the difference between my village, which has managed to get a little charity money because we're close to a city, and those that are more distant. I look on my phone and see the amount of money that is given to Minabo. I meet the local chiefs to try to get money, and they show me how little they have. There is not enough to share. The government chiefs are keeping it. And you saw how the other two villages have almost nothing. Baku's children are fighting for their lives from the moment they are born. They will carry on as the poorest people in the country and never be able to move onward. They should be given a chance."

Jessica nodded slowly, aware that all eyes, all hopes, were on her. "Thank you for showing me what you need, and for explaining what's going on. You're right. Things must change." How she was going to make that happen, she wasn't sure. But she was sure that she had to find a way.

"My son believes we should revolt," Mukasa said. "That we should encourage the population to say we have had enough and have a peoples' uprising. I believe that will achieve nothing, that many people will die. And I believe that any person who manages to take the power from the government will see the wealth that is available to them, and they will forget where they came from, and become just like the people they took down."

A lot of shouting ensued. Jessica could only make out a few words, but the sentiment was clear. Anger was simmering. How long until it boiled over?

"Quiet. I have nearly finished." Mukasa motioned, and the area went silent. "I believe that we need someone like the ambassador to tell the world what is happening here, and that it will embarrass our government into putting the money where it should be. They would have to *show* how they have added facilities and invested money into the people, and it will be clear they have been lying. Only then will things begin to change." He looked at Jessica, his eyes kind. "Will you help us, Madam Ambassador? Will you help us get the message to the world that we need help, and that the money from your country is all going to crooked men?"

Jessica blinked back tears and looked around. "I will do everything in my power to help. I swear it." Silence followed her statement for a long moment, then Mukasa nodded before he said something else to the gathered crowd. The general conversation was loud as the audience of several hundred villagers lapsed into discussion.

Mukasa squatted beside her. "We will have another meeting tomorrow when we will hear my son speak about why we should move in his direction instead of mine. Now, we will eat and drink."

Jessica took a deep breath. She'd hoped his rallying speech was the final word. But now it was clear that the villagers were going to be given a choice: to release her or kill her. She stopped herself from dry retching. Her heart beat so loudly, it made her head ache. She might only have one day left to live.

One day, and so many regrets.

There was so much she would leave undone. She was just getting her political mojo back, and she was sure that she could get the message to both the press and the governments to let people know what was happening here. She just needed to live to do it.

CHAPTER TWELVE

Alex ate with a couple of the commission staffers and enjoyed a pleasant couple of hours listening to stories of the "old" Africa that she'd been a part of when she was learning her trade. She returned to her temporary office and decided to catch up on the latest briefings from London and her personal email. She began to read a note from Flick and leaned back in her chair when she had to read it twice.

Who was she kidding? She was going through the motions; she wasn't paying attention. She'd spent the day full of anger and disbelief. Disbelief that one of her subordinates had walked out, leaving no information as to her whereabouts, which was both dangerous and stupid. A white woman, even one built like Mitch, heading out alone was foolish. Didn't the ambassador's situation prove that? It was only a chance conversation on the way back from the president's house that meant she wasn't out of her mind with worry.

Thomas, the chauffer, had said, "It was lucky that Eric has a motorbike he's not using today, and he was happy to do a deal with Miss Mitch, so that she could run her errands."

"What?" She'd clenched her fists, then took a breath. "Oh yes, her *errands*."

"She told Eric she'd be back around nine o'clock," Thomas had said.

But the more time that had passed, the more she'd inwardly ranted and raved. Her emotions were off the scale in both directions, rage and passion. In the middle, there was space for a little worry that Mitch was safe. Alex didn't need this kind of insubordination on a mission this important. Routine, order, plans... They'd agreed, damn it. This was exactly what Alex had been worried about. *Cowboy Americans.*

But what should she do about it? Mitch had already told her she acted without thinking it through, which she'd clearly done here. Or, if Mitch *had* thought things through, she'd decided that the slow Brit would thank her for getting on with the op.

There was a shadow in the doorway, and Mitch came in, all swagger and sex.

She held up her hands. "I know you're going to be pissed with me for going behind your back, but I have an excuse."

"I'll be interested in hearing it," Alex said, gripping the arms of her chair tightly.

"I wasn't achieving anything sitting about here waiting for the president to see us, and I thought it would be a better use of my time to liaise with the contractors and find out what supplies they needed. Did I miss anything?"

Alex blinked, the moment seeming somewhat surreal. "You *haven't* missed me being incandescent with rage. I'm struggling to think of the words that might allow me to have a conversation with you."

"Incandescent, huh?" Mitch leaned against the doorframe, and her gaze moved over Alex like a caress. "It looks good on you."

Alex gripped the chair even tighter and closed her eyes. Okay. So Mitch was prepared for a blow-out. That meant Alex shouldn't give her one. *Professional. Focus.* "The meeting with the president went as we expected. He had nothing new to tell me and insists the ambassador will turn up eventually. No surprise there." Her voice was a little tight and her words clipped, but she held her anger.

Mitch raised her eyebrows and nodded.

"Since you've already risked life and limb to meet our assets, tell me about the setup. I want to go with you tomorrow, preferably not on the back of your borrowed motorbike." Though, if they weren't on a mission, that might be a pleasant way to spend a few hours, hugging Mitch tight. She shook it off and huffed out a breath. "But right now, I want you to tell me how you'd do things differently next time. You said you needed to learn to think before you move, and yet you acted today without any thought whatsoever for our professional relationship. You made mistakes, and I'd like to know if you can recognize them." She winced inwardly at her waspish tone.

Mitch put her hands in her pockets and was silent. She looked at a spot over Alex's head, her head tilted like she was thinking about something and looking like a recalcitrant schoolgirl stood in front of the head mistress. It certainly felt that way from Alex's side.

Mitch took her hands out of her pockets and looked at Alex. She started counting off her mistakes using her fingers. "I'm not sure whether it's a mistake, but I involved Eric by borrowing his bike. It could have got trashed, or I could have lost it and that would've been bad because he really needs it. I didn't do any of those, so in a way, it was a mistake that wasn't."

"I don't want the reasons or the excuses; I just want you to recognize the errors." Alex said. This was going to be more difficult than she'd expected. But at least Mitch hadn't stormed off. If Mitch wanted the promotion, she had to learn.

"Two, I didn't discuss anything with you. That could have been three, four, and five as well, because I didn't tell you where I was going, what I was doing, or how I was getting there. And by just leaving, created a headache for you. Six, I didn't attend the president meeting, although I didn't miss anything, and you handled it like the pro you are. I think that's everything."

"Seven," Alex said, "you risked your life heading out into the city and beyond. It could have been *you* being kidnapped or shot. Eight, if you'd taken too long, or I hadn't found out you were on Eric's bike, I could have risked more lives by sending people out looking for you."

"Okay. I get it." Mitch briefly dropped her gaze to the floor.

"It's not so much about you risking your life. You need to

think about the consequences of things going wrong, or of circumstances changing. I get that you've always had just yourself to focus on, and that you have survival skills that have been finely honed on the streets of the US and Mexico. But you need to start considering others who get drawn into your adventures."

"Okay, Alex. I get it. I do. I'm sorry." Mitch shoved her hands in her pockets again, all sign of her swagger gone. "And you're pissed that I didn't go along with the plan we talked about. I didn't want to risk you saying no because if you did, I would have had to go against your orders."

"Why didn't you wait another day or two? What was the hurry?" Alex tried to breathe slowly. *Calm. Professional. Focus.*

"I needed something to do, and I wanted to be able to see what they had, so that I could get on with the planning. I could've waited a day, I suppose. If I had, I wouldn't be standing here explaining myself. Alex, every day we waste is another day the ambassador could be killed, if she's even still alive, which isn't something we've discussed. Standing around with our thumbs up our butts isn't helping."

"But now we have to do the same thing again tomorrow," Alex said. Clearly Mitch's apology was more about cutting the conversation short. She couldn't let Mitch have the upper hand. Alex wanted to see the US assets for herself and make sure they accepted her leadership. That was non-negotiable.

"Yes, and that would be one more thing in Leadership 101." Mitch ran her hand through her hair. "Make strategic decisions that save both time and energy."

Alex gave up. They weren't going to see eye to eye on this one. "Tell me about the US assets we have and what we can expect from them. Do we need to obtain anything for them? Weapons or ammunition? Vehicles, etcetera?"

"They're self-sufficient and have their own lines of supply," Mitch said, her shoulders dropping a little. "They can provide us with everything we need, and their scouts are already out searching for intel. Once we have an objective, we can make a detailed plan with them. They've worked here for a few years and have a covert existence."

Alex nodded slowly. "Have they had any intelligence yet about where the ambassador might be? Anything that might help us?"

"They have two or three informants in the north who'd all heard whispers of something happening, but there's nothing of any value yet." Mitch leaned against a filing cabinet. "They hoped to get reports in by tomorrow and would let me know, but another visit would be better than waiting for a phone call."

"Will our showing up tomorrow cause them problems? Won't we need some kind of cover?" Alex asked.

"I'll talk to Green and see what he thinks." She looked Alex over. "Me showing up on a bike wasn't noticeable. You, though… Yeah, you'd stand out." She grinned when Alex rolled her eyes. "We should get a car that's a bit of an old beater, so we can take it to their garage to fix."

"Okay. Until tomorrow," Alex said. "And Mitch, don't mess with this mission or disobey my command again. If you do, I'll have to ask your government to send someone else."

Mitch's eyes darkened. She gave a sharp salute, then turned and left without a word.

Alex sighed and rubbed at her temples. Why were hot woman always such a pain in the backside?

The next morning, after an awkward, silent breakfast, Mitch went on a hunt for the kind of vehicle they needed.

Mitch appeared an hour later, dangling a set of car keys. "Someone was happy to hire out his car for the day. He filled the tank, and we won't reed to touch it. Are you ready?"

Alex had to admit that seeing Mitch in motion was sexy, though she shoved that thought aside quickly. Mitch always had a foot outside the lines, and that was the reason some of her operations as leader came unstuck. Alex wasn't certain that she'd be able to convince her to stick to the rules, but she'd have a damn good try.

The journey out of the city was an eye-opener. The combined stench of sewage and diesel fumes was overwhelming enough, but the noise of the people shouting created a cacophony that could implode Alex's head. She let Mitch drive, and they traveled in silence until they reached the garage. A man with neck tattoos and kind eyes waved them inside. Mitch introduced the guy as Blue, and they headed to the back before following a path to the goldmine. Even though Mitch had explained the cavern, Alex was still surprised at the size of the place and the amount of machinery in it.

"Good morning. You must be Alex," a voice said from somewhere in the cavern.

A smiling man came from the depths wearing shorts and a tank top, and he was covered in sweat.

"Yes, and you're Green?" Alex said. She looked him over and decided he looked fit enough for the job.

He winked, as if he'd clocked her perusal. "As soon as you can give us some idea of where the ambassador is being held, we'll be ready to move. I know you'll want to plan the final details, but we have the manpower and equipment."

"It's likely to be a long distance over difficult terrain," Alex said. "What are the vehicle arrangements?"

"We have a couple of jeeps and trucks, but I expect we'll need to fly to cover the distance quickly. We'll probably have to cover the savannah on foot if she's being held in certain open areas. But I have contacts in the north who can rent us a truck or two. Because we think she's likely to have been taken north, we've sent some things in advance."

"Your job seems to be as much about your network of contacts as managing men and kit," Alex said.

Green nodded. "I need to be able to provide the right kit and the right people for whatever Uncle Sam might need and, as with your work, it's nearly all off the books."

"Well, color me impressed," Alex said. "As Mitch probably said, we haven't had any help from the Minabo government, although the British High Commissioner is using her contacts to see if she can find anything. I wanted to meet with you to see your setup and to find out if you've had any new information coming in since yesterday. Mitch said you were expecting some reports."

"We have a number of informants out, particularly in the northern villages, since that's where the whispers say she is. We've been waiting for some information that we can act on, so that we don't waste our time." Green rolled his shoulders. "And last night, we only got rumors in our intelligence. We have a man contacting us later today, and we're hopeful. He's in a town near one of the villages, and he keeps his finger on the pulse. The problem with the villages on the savannah is they're spread out, and the contact between villages is sporadic. What we could use are some decent maps of the north. Can you get your hands on any up-to-date mapping?"

"I'll see what we can do. Between your informants and the High commissioner's informants, hopefully we'll hear something soon. Once we have word, we'll let you know and can meet up with you to put together any final details before we move."

Green showed them both around the setup, before they returned to the garage and picking up their car. One of the troops gave them a bill and asked for a cash payment. "We changed your oil, plugs, and air filter."

Alex looked at Mitch, who pulled a handful of screwed-up Minabo and US dollars from her pocket.

"I'll take those dollars you have there if it's okay with you," the mechanic said, already picking his way through Mitch's stash.

As they drove back to Solunwa, the atmosphere became one that Alex liked. Mitch appeared relaxed, and Alex decided that she was trying to do the right thing and play the leadership game. Maybe the rest of the operation would work out just fine.

CHAPTER THIRTEEN

LATER THAT EVENING, MITCH sat in the lounge at the British High Commission with a beer. She sighed, trying to stem her frustration at not being able to actively move the situation along. She didn't think things through properly and worked using her instincts. She liked it that way, when her instincts were on point, and everyone was grateful because she saved lives or got good results.

But sometimes her instincts were off, and she fucked up, and they'd lose men or weapons and not get the result they needed. Paddy said to think through the risks before taking big leaps. If there was a big risk, make sure it was worth it, but losing lives was rarely worth it. He had a job for her as a captain; she just had to show he could trust her.

Mitch bristled, and her body tensed as she went through her dressing down from Alex yesterday. Why couldn't she realize they were wasting time? Mitch took a swig from her beer and calmed herself down. Her thoughts would change nothing, and she had to move forward. But damn it all...

Alex came in and joined her. "Another beer?"

"Yeah, please." Mitch took a final gulp and handed the glass to her.

Alex came back with their drinks. "I'd forgotten how the heat seems never ending. I could do with an hour or two on the Norfolk coast in a cool breeze this evening."

"I wouldn't mind some time there myself. That is, if you'd still invite me?"

"I would if I thought you might take me up on the offer." Alex gave her a small, wary grin.

Mitch leaned back in her seat and looked into Alex's eyes. "Ask me again when we have the ambassador safe and sound."

Alex stared straight back. "I will."

There was a moment's silence, filled with things Mitch couldn't say aloud. She stared into Alex's eyes, which made her think about sunny days and a life yet to be lived. *Stop it.* Poetic thoughts led to stupid decisions. She just wanted a few nights of passion.

"We have the whole evening in front of us. Tell me where you're from. Who were you as a kid?" Alex took a sip of her wine.

"Okay, this is where you get to know the rest of your team. Me today, the assets tomorrow?" Mitch's chest was tight, and her jaw ached. She was just part of the job Alex needed to do, wasn't she?

"I'm not being intrusive. I mean, I don't intend to be. I'm sorry it's nothing to do with work. I just wanted to get to know a bit about you. I really know nothing."

Mitch shrugged. "I don't really tell people about my early life. It wasn't exactly good, and people make judgments, you know. About where you're from and what you've done."

"I know about that in some respects. I didn't go to university, because I'd joined the army to get away from home. But it's surprising how many people I meet in work and socially that look down their noses at me when they find out I don't have a university education." Alex ran her hand through her hair. "You can tell me anything, and I won't judge you."

Mitch had never spoken about her childhood to anyone, but for some reason, she wanted Alex to know. Maybe Alex gave her a safe space. "I missed a lot of school when I was young and was always catching up."

"Were you sick?" Alex asked.

"That would've been a better reason. I was raised in the mountains in West Virginia, and we had no money and didn't need educating, according to my family. Especially the girls."

"That's hard to understand when you were living in a country where education is free and attendance is compulsory," Alex said.

"Yeah, well, there's only so much the state can do if a family doesn't care about sending their kids to school. And then, when I was thirteen, I found my uncles who lived with us were staring at me, winking and whispering to each other." She pushed her glass around on the beer mat. Why had she started down this road? It would explain things to Alex, and she could understand her a little better, but this was her big secret and telling it made her defenseless. "I worked out what was going to happen if I stayed there. They'd wait until everyone was out, and I'd be theirs. So I ran away." She shivered. She didn't want pity; she just needed a sense of closeness with someone.

"I'm sorry. That must have been so hard. How did you leave?"

"Everyone was watching a Steelers' game and drinking beer. It was late afternoon, and I knew I wouldn't be missed 'til morning. I left with the clothes I had on and twenty bucks I stole from my mother. I knew they'd likely look for me within about twenty miles and after that, they wouldn't bother, so I took a bus right to the end of the line. I spent the next year living on the streets and ended up in Orangeville, Baltimore."

"Oh my God," Alex said. "How did you survive?

"Fist fights and determination. Anything was better than what would happen at home."

Alex sighed and bit her lip. "I don't think I can ever understand your life on a real level. I've been lucky. I've always had a roof over my head, food and clothing. To be without it..."

Mitch shivered, remembering those days trying to stay alive and fighting for everything. "Orangeville was where I met my honorary mom, Sue. She was a cop who found me trying to get a drink from a vending machine with a knife. She came over holding out a five-dollar bill." Mitch smiled at the vivid memory that had become part of her soul. "I remember looking at her, not sure whether it was a trap and wondering whether my thirst would overcome my fear. She said I could keep the change, which would've fed me for a week, but she wanted to know what I was going to do with it. I told her I'd buy bread and jelly and save anything left over for the next day."

"My God, you must've been starving. It's amazing you survived." Alex put her hand on Mitch's arm.

"She asked if I had somewhere to live, because I always looked clean and tidy. But I clammed up. There was no way I was going to talk to a cop. I've never forgotten what she said: 'Okay, I know how this goes. You say nothing, I insist on knowing. You get bristly, and I get angry. You run, thinking I'm going to put you in care.' She was dead right, of course. I was within an inch of running."

"Fear of staying but frightened of running back to the dread of everyday living." Alex shook her head. "I can't even imagine."

"Sue told me she had a couple of rooms at the back of her house her mother used to live in, and they'd be private. I could move in and have my own front door. I'd never met anyone who was giving away something for nothing before. I asked her what the catch was and got ready to run. I told her I had no money so I couldn't pay her, I didn't do any funny business with sex or whatever, and I was mostly honest. I waved my knife and said I could look after myself. She just smiled." Her eyes welled with tears, and she cleared her throat. She wouldn't cry in front of Alex. "Sue said that I could go to school or college if I had an address and someone to vouch for me. She believed she could help me make a future. She gave me the five dollars and told me to think about it." She laughed lightly. "I didn't need to think for long. I was starving. I was spending a lot of time defending myself against men or hiding from them. I had to keep moving my little tent made from plastic sacks, and it took most of my day to find enough to eat and somewhere to sleep. I wanted to have a safe place to call home. I told her I wanted it, there and then. If it went bad, I'd just take off again. That day I had money, a home, and an honorary mom. Sue got me into high school, organized remedial classes to help me catch up, and taught me that life didn't have to be about fighting all the time. I went to karate and taekwondo classes to help lose some of my anger." She took a deep, steadying breath and a long drink of her beer. What had possessed her to share all that?

"Thank you for telling me. I know that it must've been hard for you to talk about," Alex said.

Alex moved her hand from Mitch's arm, and she felt the separation immediately. "I've never told anyone about that. I call her Momma because I love her just like a mom even though we aren't related."

Alex sighed deeply. "I thought I had it bad when my parents didn't understand me being a lesbian, but I can't imagine what you've been through. You took control and defied the odds." She shook her head. "That's really inspirational."

"Yeah, well, I don't dwell on it. But that's the kind of adult I am too. I like to take control and be in motion."

Alex changed the conversation to what they'd seen of Solunwa, and Mitch was relieved that nothing seemed to have changed between them. Theoretical situations and practicalities were thrown out and set aside, and eventually Alex was yawning more than talking, and they separated for the night. Mitch watched her leave, wishing she was going with her. Instead, she made her way to her own room and fell asleep quickly, hoping to dream of Alex's soft lips and her long hair caressing Mitch's skin.

She woke suddenly to the low vibration of her phone. "Yeah?" Mitch looked at the time. Who the hell was calling her at one a.m.?

"Green. We've got information about a location. Our contact had some good information. Some men were in a bar, talking about the chief of the nearby village being weak for not wanting to kill the white woman, and how that was about to change. We're all set and ready to extract. Do you want to involve your boss?"

"No," Mitch said. "It'll be good to have a US operation to rescue the US ambassador," Mitch said.

"Do *you* want to be involved?" Green asked.

"Yeah, I'll sneak out." She swung her legs out of bed and turned on the light.

"Okay, I'll pick you up on the way. The rest of the team will head straight for the planes and start loading up. See you in about twenty minutes."

As Mitch was getting dressed, she revisited her reasoning for not involving Alex. She wanted to be able to bring in this whole operation for her country. The Brits seemed to have taken over the whole thing, and she wanted to give Uncle Sam the win. *Her* ambassador. *Her* problem.

On a personal level, it wouldn't be great for their relationship. A small voice at the back of her mind reminded her that she had a connection to Alex, and this would likely to be the end of it. *All's fair in love and war*. She wasn't going to miss this chance.

She slid away through the High Commission grounds and out the gate. She nodded to the sentries and as she emerged onto the road, Green slowed to a stop on his motorbike and picked her up. Mitch couldn't shake the feeling that she should call Alex and tell her what was going on. But she didn't. That would only slow things down, and she needed this op to be hers and hers alone. Maybe Alex would understand that when they were on the other side of it. Thanks to the hour, traffic was almost non-existent, and they made good time to the local airstrip.

Green took them to the back of a tin hut on the side of the runway where he hid his bike. The plane was ready on the runway, engines running, lights on, and someone in the pale light of the cockpit. Mitch smiled as she climbed on board the plane, welcoming the adrenaline rushing around her body. This was what her life was all about.

Once they were airborne, they worked on a detailed plan, and Mitch looked at Green's map.

He pointed to a mark on the low-scale map. "We land here at the airstrip, and this is the road we'll take to the village."

"I don't want us too close. We need to maintain the element of surprise," Mitch said. "I'd rather we create an envelope, moving in here and here." She pointed to the two sides of the village.

"Agreed."

"It looks like there are a number of different enclosures here, each clearly marked."

Green nodded. 'The chief has different areas for different wives. His families and other villagers spread out from there. Pretty sure this area here is the number one wife's enclosure, which is where the ambassador will be held. She's valuable property, and the prestige of holding her is important. That leaves us with the problem of getting in and out without being noticed, and if the ambassador is there, getting her out safely."

Mitch traced the lines through and outside the village with her fingertip, picturing the movement. "Everyone should be asleep. We follow this path through the shower and latrine areas, up from the river. We'll miss most of the villagers and reduce the risk of getting noticed, until we get into the main domicile area. Then we'll have to find the ambassador and get her out without waking anyone else."

Green gave a low whistle. "The timing is going to be close. If we're delayed anywhere, we'll have to call it off and keep watch for twenty-four hours before going in. Otherwise, we have to do it in daylight and cause a shitstorm."

"I don't want to do that," Mitch said. "There's too much at stake right now." It would also cause problems with Alex and the Brits if things went sideways, and she didn't get the ambassador out. Maybe she should've brought Alex along to talk the villagers into letting the ambassador go. "Are you good with the plan? You have the experience in this theatre, and I'm relying on your feel for the ground. If it's not a go, tell me now."

"Yep, this is good." Green straightened. "I'll brief the guys when we land. Then we can head out."

They were soon coming in to land. Mitch's heart pounded, and the adrenaline flooded her system, the typical pre-operation feeling that she thrived on; it was a narcotic better than any drug. It overpowered any fear, but that gave her time to think about Alex. Where could she fit into this? Maybe this was why she struggled to understand how she and Alex could be together in anything more than a casual way. Like the men around her, she was trained for action, not a lot of chitchat. Just as they'd chosen to stay in the field instead of going home, she couldn't imagine being rooted anywhere. *Damn it*. She had a quiet thought about her nightmares but did what she usually did when she started to see things she wanted to forget: blanked them and focused on the mission ahead.

The plane landed on a darkened strip, throwing up dirt and rocks that hit the windows. Nothing else mattered now. Not the politics, not Alex's disappointment, not the promotion. Now she needed to rescue a woman in need, and she'd get it done.

They were met by two trucks stripped down to a base coat with a wood bed.

"As I said to Alex yesterday, I expected that we'd come north with her disappearing so completely. I sent a couple of guys ahead with trucks and some of the heavier arms which we may not need, but it's good to have them up there in case. The village we're looking for is quite a few miles from the landing strip, but it should only take a couple of hours," Green said.

The soldiers disembarked from the plane once it had pulled over to the side of the runway and everyone headed for the two trucks. There were two men already there, in the uniform of Green's mercenaries, along with a small red-haired man, who nodded at Green.

"Hey, Jock. The ambassador still with number one wife?" Green said.

"I wouldnae know. They may've already gone," Jock said.

Mitch squinted into the darkness as she parsed out the words from his broad Scottish accent.

"You're coming with us?" Green asked.

"Aye, I'll take you there. I know the shortcut."

Green outlined their plan. He passed a copy of the map to three of the men, who looked at the details with dimmed flashlights. They'd discussed the map before leaving their HQ, and Green told them Mitch's plan for an envelope infiltration with a quiet extraction. Blue's squad would provide the backup along the route and maintain a presence to allow Green's squad to enter the number one wife's area. There were nods all around.

Mitch clapped her hands lightly. "This woman is American and allowing one of ours to be taken without rescue or reprisals is not how our country works. We get in, grab our target, and get out. I don't expect us to use more force than necessary but look out for villagers who want to become celebrities for killing an American soldier. Go and good hunting."

The two squads separated, and Mitch followed Green and his squad into the back of one of the trucks. Jock went into the front with the driver. The journey was rough in the back of the truck; there was little that could be described as a road, and the tracks through the grasslands were rutted and muddy in places and sandy in others. As she bounced around in the back, focusing on the op, thoughts of Alex continued to intrude. *Fuck.* Should she have woken Alex up and brought her with? Or would she have insisted on notifying everyone and their grandmother first? Mitch had to believe she'd chosen the right option, but she was damn sure Alex wouldn't see it that way.

They stopped, and both squads left their vehicles. There was silence as the men got into a well-rehearsed formation. Mitch slotted into Green's squad, and they set off on a ruck march, staying low and silent. They'd covered around three miles when Jock stopped them. The river was ahead, and the silent village appeared against the horizon.

Mitch followed Green along the side of the river, and the squads separated out into the surrounding trees. They went past the latrine area, easily identified by the rank stench, which made Mitch's eyes water. Green led the squad in through the fences made of tree branches and toward the huts. The light was just beginning to break, making it possible for Mitch to see the two open-sided huts and the mosquito-netted bodies inside.

Only one hut contained children, and Mitch guessed the women were with them. The rest of the squad surrounded the other hut, assuming it was a men's hut. Mitch held up her fist, and Green's team stopped in place. She lowered it slowly, and then moved in by herself, scanning the prone bodies.

A child snuffled and rolled over, and she froze, making no sound, until the child curled up and settled down again. She breathed a sigh of relief and continued to move around the sleeping forms. She made a full circuit and did one more scan. *She's not here. Fuck me, she's not here.* She left the hut and signaled to the rest of the team. One of them scoped the second hut and came out, thumb down. They looked in the cooking hut and the other huts to discover they were empty of people. The whole thing was a bust.

She nodded at Green, who raised his hand and motioned for them to move out. They left the enclosure, and as they got down to the river, a shot was fired from the other bank. There were several more shots fired, and Blue's squad, who were providing a rearguard, responded.

The night lit up with gunfire.

Green's team melted into the trees and hoofed it back to the trucks. Mitch turned at one point to see one of the soldiers behind her take a bullet to the upper thigh. There was a sudden flower of blood on his trouser leg, and he went down.

His buddy pulled him further into the trees and quickly applied a tourniquet. Another soldier took his backpack, another his machine gun, while a third tossed his own backpack on the ground and made a stretcher from it. The men put the wounded soldier onto it, and they followed the rest of the team, moving quickly. There was still gunfire from the rest of the rear party, but it got more sporadic as they retreated to regroup at the trucks.

"So that was bad," Mitch said, stating the obvious. "I'd hoped we'd get in and out without being spotted."

Green rolled his eyes. "No shit. I'm not sure who spotted us, but I assume it was a returning cattle-herding party."

"The herders are armed too?" Mitch was pissed at herself for not considering that *everyone* was armed in this part of the country.

"A lot of the men here are armed because of the government troops. The army is in the employ of the president; they're well-paid and have the best equipment. They're expected to perform and do the president's bidding. Up here in the grasslands, there's almost a war going on. The villagers' guns are outdated, but they seem to find ammunition." Green looked around, checking his men. "Maybe they're looking out for the whole village; it is the settlement of one of the main chiefs of the northern grasslands. It houses his family and his wives. Could be their sentries dozed off."

"Where did Jock go?" Mitch asked.

"He went back to the town," Green said. "He's certain she was here, but like he also said, it was possible she'd been moved before we could get here." He leaned on the truck and took a swig of water. "I still can't work out why they've taken her. If it is these people, they damn sure need the ransom money."

"I'm sure we'll find out eventually," Mitch said. The teams got into the trucks and headed off, swiftly but carefully with the injured.

"Let's get Hinch to hospital," Green said.

Hinch was pale, almost translucent. The medic on the team came over to Green.

"I don't think he'll make it, skipper," the medic said. "I applied a second tourniquet but I'm not sure it'll save him. Nicked an artery, and we can't plug it." The anguish in his eyes was plain.

She understood the horror that a colleague was dying, someone who was probably a good friend. When she saw the darker side of her job at times like these, she wondered why the hell she kept doing it. Yet she knew she'd be out there again doing the same thing in a heartbeat, just like the rest of these guys would.

Green sat beside Hinch in the rear of the truck as they headed back toward the plane. He spoke to him and listened for a short while, before bowing his head. The rest of the team was silent, still aware of their surroundings. Mitch closed her eyes. Everyone knew the risks with an op like this, but that didn't make it any easier when someone fell.

They loaded Hinch's body onto the plane and moved fast. They got airborne quickly, leaving the ground behind. Green sang "21 Guns" by Jamey Johnson, and the rest of them all joined in, the words evoking their life and the hero that Hinch had been. Mitch knew a lot of mercs who'd adopted this song to take the hurt of loss, knowing that they wouldn't be buried with full military honors, and their heroism would be unknown. Mitch ached with pride and grief. She hadn't known him, but she'd known plenty like him.

As they landed, she looked out of the aircraft over the African airstrip. Had she taken risks she shouldn't have? Would Alex be right? She didn't think so. They'd had a valid piece of information and had to act quickly. She was sure Alex didn't have the ability to move that way. Mitch had done what was needed, and if it'd been successful, it would've been lauded as a successful *US* rescue of a *US* dignitary. She sighed. Somehow, she didn't think Alex would see it the same way.

And now that it had gone to shit... Well, she had no doubt she was going to get an earful.

Mitch went back to the camp with the team and spent time learning about Hinch and his life in Africa. He'd married a local woman, and the boys were all set to go and see his wife in a village nearby.

One of the soldiers gave her a lift back to the High Commission, and she arrived back less than twelve hours after she'd left. She went straight to her room and climbed into the shower, letting the warm water soak through into her bones. The hard ruck march into the grasslands had been physically demanding, a reminder that even a few weeks out of the field could make her soft. Mentally, she was as drained as she was physically. She'd been so damn sure she could get it done and get home, victorious.

As she cinched her belt, there was a knock at her door. This was the moment she'd been expecting. "Come in."

Alex threw the door open and stood with her hands on her hips and fire in her eyes. "I've had word from Neela about an operation in the Northern grasslands where shots were fired and two villagers were injured. When I came to find you, you were missing. Tell me you weren't there. Tel me you didn't go behind my back and blow this op sky high because you just *had* to do it all by yourself."

"I can't say that." Mitch stood tall and crossed her arms. "I was there."

Alex flushed and clenched and unclenched her hands. There was a moment's silence, and Mitch vaguely wondered if Alex might actually take a swing at her.

Alex raised her hands, and her blond mane of curly hair made her look like a roaring lion. "You want to be promoted. You want to get somewhere with your career, and you want to succeed. I tell you how you can achieve that. Do not take risks. Think before you act. And you ignore it. You ignore me."

Mitch took a step backward; she was going to have to fight her way out of this. 'I had credible information from an asset. I didn't take any risks, and we had to move fast."

"Credible? If it was credible, she'd be with you right now. Instead, I could've told you that we had the same information but shortly after, we received more information that the ambassador had been moved. The same informant called later to tell us about your failed op. I would have told you this over breakfast if you'd been here instead of rushing off in the middle of the night like you don't have a boss. Like there wasn't a chain of command. Like you had the authority to do it on your own." She walked toward Mitch, who took another pace backward. "How many men were injured?"

"One man was killed." Mitch's admission was like small daggers piercing her chest.

"How many injuries? Speak up. I can't hear you." Alex came even closer.

"One man was killed," Mitch said, finally losing her temper at Alex's holier-than-thou attitude. "He died in the plane on the way back."

"And it was down to you. You okayed the mission when it was futile because *you* knew better." Alex got in Mitch's face. "Do you understand yet? His death was your fault. You didn't need to go on that mission. If you'd been the leader, you would've understood that it was necessary to wait a beat for any other information. And you would've had the team to do it properly."

"My fault?" Mitch asked. "I agreed the mission with Green."

"You're paying Green; he doesn't make the decisions. You should have waited for all the facts, and you should have discussed it with me, the *actual* team leader. But no, you went off half-cocked. Because of that, a man is dead and his family will be grieving." Alex prodded Mitch's chest. "Not to mention you've now alerted the kidnappers that we're out searching for the ambassador, and you may have cut our time to save her in half. If she isn't already dead because they don't want to get caught with her in their village. You've potentially made it ten times harder to find her, dead or alive." Alex finally seemed to run out of breath, and she closed her eyes.

"I'm sorry." Mitch hung her head. She'd wanted a bit of glory for Uncle Sam and a bit of glory for herself. If it had worked, she would've been a hero. As it was, she'd fubared the mission completely.

Alex opened her eyes, the dark circles under them clearer as the sun came through the window. "Don't say sorry to me; you need to say sorry to the family. I want you to find out where the family are and go see them. Make sure they understand what a hero their son, husband, or brother was. Make it clear he did an excellent job. Get any particulars you need to in order to make sure we can take care of the family, if he's still got military employ. But know deep down that he'd still be alive if you'd just followed commands." Alex turned and walked toward the door, then she stopped. "I can't talk anymore, because I'm not even sure you're hearing me. You've let yourself down, you've let your uniform and country down, and you've let me down. I'm not sure I'll ever trust you again." She jerked the door open and stalked out.

Mitch stood for a long while, rooted to the spot by Alex's disappointment. She stared at the door and tried to think of something, anything, rather than the look on Alex's face.

Crying was a waste of time, but fuck, she wanted to, which was irritating. Life had become super difficult since she'd met Alex Hartley; there was no disputing the fact. She pushed all Mitch's buttons trying to help her get to where she wanted to go. At the same time, she was trying to change her. Shouldn't a woman accept her for who she was? Trying to change someone was a losing proposition and never worth the effort. But maybe, just maybe, it could be for the better.

Mitch rested her head against the window. She *had* let everyone down, and most importantly, she'd let Hinch and his family down, just because she wanted to prove that she could do what needed to be done, and do it on her own terms. And she'd failed, proving instead that she didn't have what it took after all.

She'd do as Alex suggested and offer Hinch's wife any help they may need. At least she could do one thing Alex asked her to do. She'd blown the mission, and she could only hope she hadn't gotten the ambassador killed too.

CHAPTER FOURTEEN

ALEX HAD BEEN IN the gym for the last ninety minutes, working up a helluva sweat despite the efficient air-conditioning system. Her legs shook, and her chest burned as she ran out of energy, but her mind was still buzzing. She'd tried to exercise some of the rage away but had failed miserably. Mitch's desire to color outside the lines could very well have cost them everything.

The unauthorized op still had Alex juggling a cocktail of anger, upset, and fear. Mitch hadn't considered anyone else when she set out. There was a certain way of running operations like these to ensure that someone wasn't stuck out in the grasslands with a heavily injured member of the team. They should be able to call on medical backup if it was required and not allow someone to die needlessly. The soldier's death had been completely unnecessary.

It stung that Mitch hadn't trusted her enough to share her plans for the operation. How could she throw away their fledgling connection so easily? How could she show, so very clearly, her disdain for Alex's leadership and authority? That opened the floodgates to other worries. She'd wanted this assignment to prove herself capable in the field, but she couldn't even keep the other operative in hand, and while they now knew who had the ambassador, they still didn't know if she was alive or where she was. Mitch's actions might have pushed that stone over the cliff and caused a landslide.

And then there was the fear. That was new, and it was all about Mitch. What if she'd gotten herself killed? What if she'd been the one brought back in a body bag? That image made it harder to breathe, and she slammed the stop button on the treadmill. Yes, it was about trust, but it was also knowing that Mitch was likely to do something else without thinking through the consequences. Why would Alex even be attracted to someone like that? And yet...

By the time she was in the shower, she'd worked most of the incident through and was trying to figure out what to do next. She needed to plan ahead because if they got information, she had to ensure they could run the operation smoothly. Her thoughts on hiking through the Savannah weren't politic. Hiking was the worst thing created since dried prunes, and nothing would make her change her mind.

She went to the intelligence office within the High Commission and spoke to Neela, the operations manager. The ambassador was more at risk now that Mitch's op had failed. There was no use waiting to talk to anyone in the government. Alex was aware that they were awaiting word from their informants, and she knew that Green had informants too. Mizumbo had also said he would contact them if he had word.

So it was a waiting game. Exactly what Mitch loved least.

Alex decided they should take another trip to see Green. She wanted buy-in from everyone for any plan, and they needed reminding who was in charge. She also required everyone's knowledge of the area. Neela arranged for them to borrow one of her unit's battered Toyota undercover cars that they bought and sold often to maintain their anonymity.

And what of Mitch? She should send her back to the UK but somehow felt that she should give her a final chance. Mitch's decision-making was flawed, and she didn't consider everything in her haste to get a job done, but she might have learned something from her failed op. She was still debating when she arrived at Mitch's door and knocked.

"Yeah?"

"Good morning," Alex said, willing the butterflies to sod off because they weren't welcome anymore. *Stop.* She looked at Mitch, and her stomach dropped. "Are you unwell?"

Mitch looked dreadful. She was wearing a pair of gym shorts and a sports bra, and her face was pale. She looked as if she hadn't slept for a week. Her hair was messy, and her eyes were red. She sat on the side of her bed with her head resting in her hands, and her elbows on her knees.

"No, I'm fine." She finally looked up. "I'm just paying for my mistakes. I saw Hinch's wife and family yesterday afternoon and told them I was in charge of the op that killed their man. But they were gracious, which made me feel worse. He'd told them that life on this earth wasn't guaranteed, and that they should enjoy every moment they had together while they could. His wife said they had." She ran her hand through her hair, mussing it even more. "When I left them, I felt like I'd missed something deeply emotional in my life. They had a special relationship with Hinch, and their relationship actually made me jealous. His wife said that they spent time apart, which was hard, but they had something between them that was more than shared hopes and dreams. It was a connection on a deeper level, and their different country upbringing made it unique." Mitch stood and put her hands on her hips. "I was thinking about it most of the night." She sighed deeply and shook her head, like she was trying to dislodge the guilt. "Am I still on the team?" she asked, her tone flat and almost disinterested.

"Yes. But you need to be part of *my* team. I told you before, Mitch, I'm in charge, and what you did was unacceptable. But that's done with, so I can only hope you won't pull a stunt like that again. Hear me clearly: if you do, I will pull you from the team and send you packing without so much as a goodbye." Alex took a breath and then waved the past away. "If you can see any improvement we can make in the op or in the way I'm doing something, discuss it with me and we'll work *together*."

There was a moment's silence, and Mitch looked at her, as if she was seriously working out if this was the way she wanted to do things. Would things never be simple between them?

"Okay, will do." Mitch rolled her neck. "What's next?"

"We go over to the garage with Neela, and we tie down the plans for the operation. When we get word about exactly where the ambassador is, we can act quickly—with all of us singing from the same hymn sheet. With no delays, we can free her before something disastrous happens. Go shower and come down when you're ready."

Alex left the room quickly. This relationship needed to be on a business level first and foremost, and her desire to comfort Mitch was not on the cards today.

* * *

The drive out to the garage was silent apart from Neela highlighting a variety of retail attractions such as the shop selling only disposable razors and whose owner managed to make a good living. There was also a spice shop that had only thirty spices on sale but was thriving selling produce supplied by his neighbors and their friends. Mitch was unusually silent, and Alex hated the tension between them. It was like a piece of wool pulled so taut that some of the fibers were unraveling. She just wasn't sure how to reduce the strain.

Neela drove into the garage and got out to talk to Blue. They went through the back and followed the underground path to the caves.

"You've obviously been here before," Alex said. "I wasn't aware you knew these guys."

Neela looked over her shoulder as she continued walking. "Yes, we have a love-hate relationship. I love visiting, and they hate the kind of job I provide them with." She gave with a wry smile. "Although after yesterday, they may not want to go out again."

They arrived at the cave, where Green was waiting. Alex handed him a box file. "I have some updated maps, and we need to look at where we think the ambassador is likely to be. I understand that she originally went to Ponba and stayed with Chief Bitalo and his first wife, Lulu, when she arrived, but she's been moved on from there, as we all found out yesterday. Neela's informants have drawn a blank. Have yours come up with anything else?"

"Nothing yet," Green said. "We have a couple in the towns nearest the villages, but they've been quiet."

"Let's see if we can work out the rough area she might be in and put things in place so that we're prepared."

"I'm all for that, ma'am. We have a table set up over here. There are some bottles of Hawai, so help yourself." Green led them into a spot not too far into the cave, and they settled themselves around the table.

Alex laid out her maps, and everyone moved in to get a closer look, although Alex was aware that Mitch did so reluctantly. Was she pouting because she'd been reprimanded? Or was she upset that Alex was properly taking charge? Whatever it was, Alex shouldn't be worrying about it. But would Mitch be able to contribute to the operation? And if she did, would Alex be able to trust that she'd do the things she was supposed to?

She stared at a map of the northern savannah, thinking about how Mitch might react on the op and how she should manage her but ultra-aware that she needed to get her head in the game. This operation was complex, problematic, and a nightmare as far as the aspects of the US President and the UK Prime Minister needing to be read in on the results. They were requesting daily updates, and there'd been a lot of interest in what they were doing. Once she'd briefed Moss about the Minabo President not helping them, some of the pressure had gone. Mitch had found the same when briefing her embassy and the White House. They'd explained that Mitch's operation was carried out as a fast response to some unverified information, and that, while unsuccessful, had shown that the ambassador had probably been there earlier. At the very least, it made it clear they were close and doing their jobs. They didn't need to know it was possible Mitch had blown the whole thing.

That night back in London seemed like a dream, as did the other night when they'd shared bits of themselves, which had hinted at the possibility of something special. But the personal aspect of what they could share was clearly going to be too difficult, given their positions. And indeed, after the anger Alex had shown, Mitch might not want her anymore anyway. Her heart lurched, her stomach dropped, and nausea rolled in her gut. *Focus.*

Alex motioned toward the map. "This is the village you went to yesterday. There are a lot of other villages in the north, but most of them are farther into the savannah and will be much more difficult to get at. What tribes are here, Neela?"

Neela stared at the maps before answering. "There are several different tribes in the savannah. The main groups are the Masai, the Kikuyu, and the Dorobo. They all co-exist, although they have different cultures. The tribes in the couple of hundred miles or so of Chief Bitalo's village are all Masai. Those tribes raise cattle. The Kikuyu are traditionally farmers, and the Dorobo are hunters of small game, but there are few in the area of Chief Bitalo's village. I think we should be looking at the Masai villages. What do you think, Green?"

"Yeah, that makes sense." Green leaned on the table and looked across at Blue, who nodded. "The chief is the guy who has control of all the Masai villages, so there's a good chance he's behind this."

"I still don't get why though," Neela said. "There's only a little unrest in the villages, and that's about lack of water, medicine, and sanitary facilities."

Mitch moved forward. "Is that enough of a reason to kidnap the US Ambassador?"

Neela raised her eyebrows and shrugged. "I don't think so, unless they're making a point. Their own government does nothing to help them."

"Where would they have gone from Ponba?" Mitch asked. "It can't be that far across grasslands. There can't be many roads, so they'll be on foot."

"Good point. This village here," Alex said, tapping it, "is large and way out on its own. It looks like there's a road of sorts, but I'm not certain where it starts or where it goes to. It's not clear from the map."

"You could be on to something, Alex," Neela said. "Toluku. We know the Masai villages have used it in the past for a meeting place, because its right in the middle of Kakuku."

Green nodded. "If she's there, we'll hear about it. The informant for our last trip lives out that way, which is why he heard something about where she was."

"But not about the fact that she'd been moved," Mitch murmured, her eyes still on the map.

"The village Ponba where she was moved from, is some fifty miles from this new village," Alex said. "I don't suppose your airfield is near Toluku?"

"Nope." Green crossed his arms. "It's several miles the other side of Ponba. All the other airfields in the north are government owned."

"Is the Aerial Foundation considered government?" Neela asked. "I think they have an airfield in the northeast somewhere. It could be near this village."

"Do you know someone in the foundation who could let us know where their airstrip is?" Mitch asked. "And perhaps let us land a plane there? That plane perhaps being used on some business that is humanitarian and possibly considered illegal by the Government."

Alex smiled. The old Mitch had returned. Dangle an interesting op under her nose, and she was all in.

"I'll make some enquiries. I'm certain they are partially US-backed. The foundation funds wildlife protection and survival, and research into rare bird species." Neela looked at her phone. "No signal. Do you have Wi-Fi down here?"

"I bet they have all mod cons," Alex said, looking around once again at the impressive setup.

"We do happen to have a variety of means of communication.

At least one should be suitable for madam," Blue said in a posh English accent as if he'd been planted from a scene in Bridgerton.

He took Neela's phone and entered a password before handing it back to her. She typed quickly, and her phone buzzed several times as she received responses. "The authorized airstrip is a couple of miles from the village. There's a track between them. I assume they use villagers to help them with their work."

"That could be a problem if they hear a plane land and aren't expecting one," Alex said. "Especially if the news of last night's attack has been reported to the other villages."

No one seemed willing to break the uncomfortable silence that ensued.

"I'll use my little bit of influence and make sure that the villagers in Toluku don't need to follow up," Neela said. "I'll ring the village chief and explain that a Foundation plane will be landing in the next few days with some government officials on board. That should work."

Green rapped his knuckles on the table. "Okay. We need to plan that as a possibility."

Alex nodded. "I think we should land early evening and move into place as it gets dark if your trucks are still up there and can take us closer. We should move into place on foot. Looking at the map here, if the trucks take us to this spot using this track that comes from the airstrip, we can move in to hide in our position here."

"Yeah," Green said, "the trucks are still up there, and I like your plan."

Alex smiled. "Good. I'd like to ensure that we don't lose the ambassador if she's here. So we need to block off all possible exits."

"While Blue's team did a great job in Ponba, it would be good to have Green backing up and covering all the exits, and Blue approaching the village with Alex and myself." Mitch pointed to the map. "There are more exits in this village, and I think Green will be better used on the perimeter if things come up."

Blue's team had just lost Hinch, and despite being professionals, it was clear Mitch thought that giving them a different job this time would be better.

"What do you guys think?" Alex asked. "I'm happy to go with whatever you suggest."

"Yep, suits me," Green said. "You okay, Blue?"

Blue nodded. "Yeah, so we go in here and check these places here for the ambassador." He tapped on each location within the village. "How did you get such detailed maps?"

Neela put a finger to her nose. "I can't say."

Everyone chuckled. In the intelligence community, contacts were sacred.

"What do we need in the way of arms and ammunition?" Alex asked.

"We have everything you and Lieutenant Brennan are likely to need," Green said.

"The HK416 you gave me was perfect for the last op. Have you shot one, ma'am?' Mitch asked.

Though there was nothing in her expression to suggest she was being sarcastic, the distance in her tone made Alex ache a little. "Yes, on my last op. It was a little heavier than I was used to but otherwise good. I'll be happy if that's what you supply us. May we both have Glocks as well?"

"Sure thing." Green nodded to Blue, who acknowledged the silent order. "We'll make sure they're loaded in. I'll give you the ammo today so you can load it into your assault packs."

"Does anyone have a guide or informant who can take us into the village, just in case there are guards, etcetera? I'd prefer to know what's likely in advance if that's possible." Alex said.

"We have a contact in the village, but he hasn't talked to us in a very long time," Neela said. "I'll check with his handler and see what she thinks. I'll let you know the result."

"I wonder if I should go back to the president and see if he can be persuaded to help.' Alex drummed the table with her fingers. "We might get some results. He may send in some troops to help us."

"Ma'am, I would suggest we wait for informants," Neela said, her eyes wide, and her hands clenched. "If the government troops come north, there will be a blood bath, with indiscriminate killings of women and children."

"I agree with Neela." Green shoved his hands in his pockets and shook his head. "It'll get very ugly if we involve troops. They shoot first and ask questions later. Our way is much better. We're much more likely to find the ambassador and get her out alive without government *assistance*."

Alex was silent for a moment as she considered that. "Okay. I accept your advice. Anyone got anything to add?" When no one responded, she said, "We need to consider what we'll do if the ambassador isn't here, and we miss her again." She looked around the table, and everyone began talking at once, so she held up her hand, and they fell silent. Thank God they were finally recognizing her leadership. "Green, you first."

"If she's not in this village, then she's likely to be somewhere in another local Masai village. We find Chief Bitalo and the Council of Chiefs and put pressure on them to help us. It will need your diplomacy and the weight of our arms behind it."

Neela nodded. "I think that's a good plan for now. We need to stay flexible."

"Mitch, what do you think?" Alex asked.

Mitch looked up quickly, as if she wasn't expecting the question. "I think Green has the right idea. We just need to be careful about any of the armed villagers who'd rather kill us than return the ambassador."

"Very well. We wait for word of sightings of the ambassador and hope our intel is good. If not, we have enough information to adapt. This time, please don't make a move without letting me know what's going on." Alex looked around the table, meeting people's eyes, all except Mitch, who seemed to find something interesting about her boots. "Yesterday's mess ended with Hinch dead. And we don't know if innocent villagers were killed too. We simply *can't* afford that kind of chaos again. As it is, we're on politically unstable ground, and we may have already cost the ambassador her life by forfeiting our stealth position and any goodwill we could've built with diplomacy. Understood?"

There were nods all around and a couple murmured, "Yes, ma'am."

As they headed back to their car, Alex hoped that this op would be successful. She thought of the poor ambassador, who'd been in the hands of the kidnappers for ten days. Alex had worked enough missions saving women in need to know it didn't always work out the way she wanted it to. As she, Mitch, and Neela got back in the car, she met Mitch's gaze for a moment. It was haunted and guarded. She couldn't bear it, so she looked away.

Alex sighed and stared out the window. If being in command meant keeping people at a distance, maybe she wasn't really cut out for it.

CHAPTER FIFTEEN

MITCH HADN'T BEEN THIS conflicted since she was back in basic training. She always knew what the sensible thing to do would be, but she could often see a much better way. One that wasn't sensible but was quick and efficient. In basic, she'd come unstuck a couple of times as she tried to get around a rule or procedure to get better results. On the whole, it'd worked. It was only when things went wrong that she'd had her ass handed to her.

And damn, Alex had kicked her ass. If the ambassador had still been in the village, she would've had no problems. *No. That's bullshit, and I know it.* She would've let down Alex whichever way she looked at it. If the ambassador had been in the village, Mitch would have been full of shit about how great the US was, and how they didn't need the Brits to get things done. Which was fine, except she was supposed to be fostering good relations, and she shouldn't have gone over Alex's head. Or behind her back. Never mind their personal relationship, which she'd well and truly blasted to hell as well. Mitch had known better, as usual, and she'd royally fucked it all up.

In her defense, she could still hear Paddy telling her not to let the Brits hold her back. But Alex hadn't held them back at all. Mitch was just going faster, getting the job done at her usual speed. She was learning though. Her usual speed was fine if she considered all angles, but because she was going fast, she cut corners. She recognized she didn't consider things fully enough. There was that job in Texas, for instance. They'd gone in to take out smugglers. They had enough men and enough weapons. It should have been enough.

What she hadn't considered was the possibility of innocents in the warehouse. The boss man and his aides managed to get control of six of the smuggled Mexicans and used them as a shield. With no knowledge of that, she'd personally killed at least one of them. When they counted up the casualties, the smugglers were dead but so were six of the people who had just been trying to get to a better life.

Mitch had vowed to try to think about the things that could be unexpected. In the op to Ponba, she hadn't considered casualties and had broken her promise to herself, yet again. *Am I really such a fuck-up?* It was becoming obvious that shit needed to change. Alex was obviously a pro at working with a team, and she made it look easy. But when Mitch had the opportunity, she'd taken a shredder to it.

She was damn lucky Alex hadn't sent her packing, along with a negative dismissal report. She needed to make it up to her. At a knock on the door, she got up and opened it. "Yeah?"

Alex entered, looking her over as though checking for grease stains. "We're on. Grab your gear, and we'll meet at the intelligence offices where Neela will tell us what she knows."

Mitch's heart stuttered and rolled into pre-operation mode, and adrenaline poured through her system. "Okay."

"I've notified the team, and they'll meet us at the airfield, ready for final briefing." Alex's eyebrow rose slightly. "I figured I'd handle that aspect before letting you know, just so everything was done in the right order. Get a move on, and I'll see you in ten."

As Mitch got ready, she couldn't help but grin as she thought of Alex. Even pissed off and distant, she was damn sexy, especially when she was giving orders and taking control. It wasn't usually something Mitch found alluring, but damn, if Alex wasn't hot as hell when she was making things happen. Mitch grabbed her go-bag and hefted it over her shoulder. This was her chance to prove to Alex that she could be a team player.

She hurried downstairs and out into the warm Minabo evening.

The air was heavy, and the disappearing light was shadowy around the trees and shrubs in the commission grounds. The remnants of red and gold light of the sunset peeked through breaks in the branches, and the background buzz of the cicadas added to the atmosphere. The sunsets here took her breath away. She stopped and laughed to herself. Alex must be bringing out the romantic in her.

Mitch arrived just behind Alex, and they were directed into the ops briefing room. The room had a number of maps of different areas of Minabo and some of the villages. A map of the northern grassland was projected onto the wall. Ponba, the village where they'd missed the ambassador in, was marked, and on the other side of the map was another mark.

Mitch looked around the room. There was a young man of Indian descent and a young Black woman with beautiful braids piled high on her head, both sitting at computer consoles. The rest of the room was empty but could probably have held twenty people without a squeeze. Obviously, operations here could be much larger.

Neela motioned for them to sit. Mitch wanted to be on the move, though, and hesitated.

Neela pointed at a chair. "The briefing is fast and short. You might want to take notes."

Mitch pulled her ops notebook from her pocket, and she sat down as directed. It had been a while since she'd been censured so politely and yet so totally.

"This is Alex Hartley from London's Department 6, and Lieutenant Mitch Brennan from the US. These two staff members have put this briefing together, so they're here in case of questions." Neela pointed to a woman. "Grace Nguzzo."

Grace stood, did a mock bow, and sat down again, smiling.

Neela gestured to the young man. "Nitin Gupta."

Nitin nodded and smiled.

"Let's begin. Ambassador Jessica Landen is being held in

Toluku, in the northern savannah," Neela said. "Grace has visited there in the guise of a member of the Aerial Foundation looking for volunteers, so I'll let her continue."

"Toluku is the capital of the Kakuku, the area the northern tribes believe is their rightful land. The village chief is one of the deputies of the chief who lives in Ponba." Grace changed the map to show the breakdown of the village. "The split is purposeful, so that the basis of power is not held solely in one place. There are four deputies spread throughout the savannah."

The map they'd seen earlier with Green and Blue wasn't as detailed. The village was large and sprawling with many enclosures, but Mitch could see the entrances and exits that they'd used in their plans, so there should be no problem there.

"However, when matters that affect all the tribes need discussion, the deputies, the chief, and other village elders meet in Toluku. Very occasionally, all the tribes meet up here, usually for ceremonial purposes." Grace turned. "Luckily for us, the meeting this time is just the chiefs and elders. That still means there are about thirty visitors who are there discussing the future of the ambassador."

"Do you know where they sleep?" Mitch asked. That information would be important since, having tiptoed around a village in the dark, she understood the problem of the presence of so many extra people and their guards.

"As far as I'm aware, most of the visitors camp outside the village, bringing their sons and grandsons with them," Grace said. "Many walk across the savannah with their cattle, getting extra food for them. They tend to stay near their herds. Most of them will be armed. Some might have modern rifles, but most have weapons that go back fifty years. They're lucky if they even fire."

Mitch clenched her jaw. "The guns around Ponba fired perfectly and were deadly."

"Yes." Grace looked directly at her. "The villagers thought they were being attacked by raiders in the night, and they fought back accordingly." She looked away. "My informant says the ambassador is with the tribal chief most of the time and has been listening to the discussions of the chiefs. They've been talking in English a lot. She also spends time with the first wife of the village chief and is likely to sleep with her and some of her daughters."

"So she's alive and being looked after to some degree." Alex nodded, looking relieved. "And if the chiefs are meeting to discuss the ambassador's future, it looks as if we're just in time. I want to get in and get her out before they decide to kill her. Will your informant guide us to the best way into the village?"

"I hope so," Grace said. "I have spoken to him, and he was rather reluctant, but I think the extra money he will earn will help deal with his fears." She pointed to the detailed map. "I've indicated that you will be entering at this entrance to the south. John Kiplagat will meet you at the only big tree a few hundred yards from that entrance. Please do not pay him, even if he asks. He earns regular money, and he can account for it. That keeps him safe."

"This map is excellent, Grace, thank you," Alex said. "I can see where we need to go internally too, should it come to that."

"Good. The pathway through the village is open and direct, and there's little cover. But these buildings are all storerooms, so you'll be safe around here. The toilet and shower is here, and I advise you stay well clear of the area this side of the village. Many of the tribes still use the open air for toileting, and the area is full of disease."

Alex looked around the room. "Has anyone had any information as to why the ambassador was abducted? It's not important for the op, but I wanted to know."

Her question was met with silence.

"Anyway. Thank you for all your efforts on this. Let's hope we're successful." Alex turned to Neela. "Thank you. Hopefully we'll enjoy a glass of something when we get back. We owe you."

Mitch followed her out of the office, and Thomas appeared in the corridor. "Macam, I have your vehicle awaiting you outside."

Within moments, they were in another battered High

Commission car and on their way to the airfield. Hopefully, Mitch could keep everyone safe and not put anyone at more risk than was necessary. She was going to enjoy this op with Alex. Though she was driving Mitch insane with her attention to detail, there was no doubting the attraction she felt. "Before we both get deep into the op, I want to tell you that I've enjoyed the prep we've done together. And I've been a damn nuisance to you, I know." It sounded formal, and a little flat, but Mitch couldn't find better words.

"I've enjoyed it too," Alex said. "We can make a good team if you get your head in the right place."

Mitch stared back into her eyes. "I'm really sorry for going my own way and not thinking about the risks to myself, you, and the op. On top of that, I put the ambassador's life and my men's lives at risk. It was wrong, and I apologize." She took Alex's hand. "Thank you for sticking with me. I promise you that I *am* learning."

Alex nodded and looked like she was going to say something but then she just gave her a quick smile and turned away.

Mitch thought about their one night together. Damn it, she wanted more time with this woman. But would she get it? Probably not, but she could dream. She shouldn't be thinking like this on her way to a dangerous op... She needed to get her head back in the game.

CHAPTER SIXTEEN

ALEX BREATHED A SIGH of relief. *So far, so good.* The plane had been an oldie but worked well and managed to fit them all in with their kit. She had briefed Green and Blue and given them maps for their teams, so they were now all up to speed. Green's trucks had moved to a hidden position near the Aerial Foundation airstrip.

The teams split into two with Green and his team in one truck and Alex, Mitch, and Blue with their team in the other. They set out along the track that led to Toluku village, and with no moor to light their way, Alex ccouldn't see a thing in the pure darkness. She shivered as the truck's dimmed headlights barely cut through the blackness.

They arrived at their rendezvous point about a mile south of the village. Green and his team jumped out of their truck, and he spoke to them quietly. Before Alex could blink, they'd headed out into the night and disappeared. She signaled her team to gather around. "We're going to wait out in the grasslands not far from the tree where Kiplagat will meet Mitch at 0200. Just before sunrise, we'll enter the village. Any questions?"

A few troops shock their heads. Mitch looked like she was going to speak, and then she just looked at the ground.

"Let's get into position. If they move the ambassador from that village, we don't want to miss it." Alex settled into her hide site to monitor the village, where there appeared to be no movement. "Blue, over," she said into her radio.

"Blue, go ahead."

"Any movement in your field of view? Over."

"Negative, over."

That was the only mechanical noise in the night. Although nighttime noise in the savannah was something different to the streets of London or even the Norfolk coast. The noise of the cicadas, loud and continuous almost like powerlines, overpowered most sounds. The other nightlife was minimal against that background tapestry: a few nightjar calls and maybe an owl. A single hyena call gave her goosebumps.

In the far distance to the west, two herders watched over the cattle, who were busy eating grass. Mitch checked in over the radio.

"Go ahead, Mitch."

"I'm going to collect Kiplagat, and then I'll bring him to your location, over."

"Good. See you in five, out."

Alex took out her night vision binoculars and watched Kiplagat creep out of the village and take a spot under the tree. She didn't see Mitch until she was next to him; her fieldcraft was excellent. They walked forward a little and then dropped to the ground. It wasn't long before they joined Alex.

"Kiplagat's happy to have a drink while we wait, so I'll pass him to Blue's team to look after." She returned minutes later and sat next to Alex.

"May I have a chat with you, please, ma'am?" Mitch asked.

Alex raised her eyebrows. Mitch had never been formal when it was just the two of them.

"I want to have an official conversation and thought this approach would be best," Mitch said then shrugged. "Obviously not."

"Go ahead, lieutenant." If Mitch wanted to move things into official territory between them, she'd keep it that way.

"I know I rush things. I cut corners and take risks, and they often cause more damage than good," Mitch said, and Alex nodded. "But I want to make the argument that we should move in early. I think we're taking a risk by being out here now, let alone hanging around for another four hours. We're too exposed."

Alex moved her legs into a more comfortable position and considered Mitch's suggestion. "Go on."

"I think that the longer we're here, the more likely we are to be spotted by one of the sentries with the cattle," Mitch said. "I think we're ready, and we should go rescue the ambassador. Now."

Alex found herself agreeing. She'd set out so early to allow for issues along the way but now that they were here, Mitch had a good point. "I agree with you, lieutenant." She wanted to encourage Mitch's thoughtful approach, but she also didn't want to come across as patronizing with someone who'd been doing seriously intense work for years. "Communicate the new plan to the team. I'll contact HQ and move everything else forward. And Mitch, good thinking."

Mitch just nodded and headed for the teams.

Moments later, they moved out, staying low. She followed Mitch, who moved like a wild cat hunting prey. She was so solid, so powerful. Alex couldn't imagine being any safer than she was behind Mitch, which was surprising given her previous actions. As they got closer, everyone halted at the sound of metal crunching underfoot. Alex watched as a tribesman walked out toward the latrines. He lit a cigarette before peeing, then headed back to the hut farthest from where they were standing.

Alex held up her fist. The guy would need to finish his smoke and hopefully fall back asleep before they could proceed. She waited five minutes until there was no more sound from that area. She signaled all clear, and the team moved forward. They checked four huts and found no women before Mitch indicated that she'd got one. Alex led her team toward it, and then they created a defensive arc around the other huts to the north. Blue created a similar arc along the south and their exit point.

She and Mitch entered the hut, but in the half-light, she couldn't make out any bodies and certainly not the ambassador. She pulled out her flashlight with red lens filters, which didn't disturb the sleepers but gave her enough to see by. The hut was stifling, despite the air from the outside coming in from the open sides. The sleeping area was full of women and children as far as Alex could see, but she couldn't identify Jessica Landen. She was going to have to do as Mitch had said and look at each person, though the mosquito nets didn't help that endeavor.

They searched quietly until Mitch put her hand in the air, and Alex moved slowly until she was alongside her. They were farthest from the entrance and had to get her past the other people in the hut, so they had to hope they just continued sleeping.

Mitch was about to remove the ambassador's mosquito net when a shot was fired.

"Shit," Alex whispered as people stirred around them, some sitting up quickly. The shots were followed by a flash bang close by, making it clear that the team behind their hut were trying to keep villagers back.

Mitch bent over the ambassador. "Ma'am, I'm with the United States government; we're rescuing you. Please come with us."

"No. No!" the ambassador shouted loudly. "I don't want to be rescued; I've got work to do."

"I'm sorry, ma'am, but you have to come now." Mitch grabbed hold of the ambassador and pulled her toward the exit.

Alex scanned the villagers and children to make sure they didn't have weapons. "Everyone, please stay where you are, and you won't get hurt." She repeated the warning in Swahili. "We've come to take the ambassador home."

Alex followed the ambassador and Mitch into the melee outside, and they hurried her out of the village.

"You're safe now, ma'am, we'll look after you. You'll be home in a few days."

Mitch's impatience was clear as the ambassador continued to tug against her.

"I have to stay," the ambassador said.

Alex looked over her shoulder to see their teams providing

defensive cover with just a few rounds and a number of flash bangs to keep the villagers away.

"Boss, over,"

"Go ahead, Blue."

"Head to the brush to the south. We'll follow along and tidy up behind us."

"Roger that, out." Alex motioned for Mitch and the ambassador to follow, Mitch continued to propel the ambassador forward, despite her resistance.

"I shouldn't be going with you," she said repeatedly. "I want to help them sort out their problems."

Alex went to the other side of the ambassador to help Mitch, just as two of their team pulled back to provide an escort. A couple of shots sounded dangerously close, and she and Mitch fell to the ground, pulling the ambassador with them. Their escort returned fire.

"Please stay still," Alex said. "You'll kill us all if you keep fighting us." Thankfully, it looked like the fight had gone out of the ambassador. She was still tearful and obviously emotional, but her fists had unclenched. They stayed on the ground for two or three minutes, while the fighting continued around them.

When it finally went quiet, Alex nodded to Mitch, and they got up, taking the ambassador's hands once again.

"Head for the rendezvous tree, and we can see where we stand," Alex said. They ran, staying under and around as much cover as they could. When they were there, the ambassador sank to the ground and leaned against the tree trunk.

"Are you okay, ma'am?" Mitch asked. "Are you injured?"

"No injuries, but I'm sick," the ambassador said. "I don't know why I fought you. I desperately need to get out of here. The whole thing has been so surreal, but it's good to see you." She tried to smile. "These people need help, and despite everything, they've been kind."

The radio crackled to life. "Green, over."

"What's your sitrep?" Alex asked. "Over."

"Holding a number of armed cattlemen down. Firing is sporadic. We have two casualties, minor injuries only. Will return to start location shortly."

The blue team checked in, confirming their numbers and time frame.

"Let's move out," Alex said. "Come on, ma'am, we're heading for a warm shower, clean clothes, and some decent food. And we'll get you a doctor. You'll start to feel better soon."

The ambassador smiled. "Thank you. It's good to be going home."

The return to the airstrip was uneventful, and Mitch gave Alex an encouraging smile as the ambassador walked up the stairs and into the plane.

"We did it," Mitch said, standing just a little too close and looking into Alex's eyes.

"We did." Alex suddenly found it hard to breathe in the scant space between them.

A throat clearing behind them made them move so the rest of the team could board, and Alex shook her head. *Not the time or the place.*

Or the woman.

As they strapped in and the plane rumbled down the runway, she wasn't certain that last part would hold true.

CHAPTER SEVENTEEN

For the first time in two weeks, Jessica was in a room alone, with her own breathing the only sound, but she could barely cope with where she was and what she needed to do. She was adrift in a sea of thoughts that were flowing through her mind in waves. Beth Tregawn, the British High Commissioner, had been gracious and caring. She'd escorted Jessica to the VIP suite herself and said they'd find clothing for her. The suite had a full supply of toiletries, towels, and robes that would allow Jessica to pamper herself. Yet she stood in the middle of the room unmoving, overwhelmed by the sudden change in circumstance.

The knock at the door broke her self-absorption, and she opened it, still feeling out of place.

"Here are the clothes I promised you," Beth said, her gaze searching. "Are you all right? You're looking terribly pale."

Beth being kind was perhaps the worst thing she could have done. She burst into tears, unable to handle the gentle question.

"May I come in?" Without waiting for a reply, Beth put her arm around Jessica and moved her into the room, before closing the door behind her. "Come and sit for a moment."

Once the dam burst, there was no way to stop, and Jessica sobbed uncontrollably. Beth kept her arm loosely across Jessica's shoulders, clearly understanding her need for tears and comfort. Still, crying all over a stranger wasn't exactly professional, and Jessica didn't want to upset a stiff-upper-lipped Brit. "I'm so sorry. I don't know what you must think of me."

"I think you're a strong, independent woman who has witnessed murder, been kidnapped, and held captive. And you managed to keep all your fears under wraps, not knowing if and when rescue would come. Now you can let all your feelings out. I'm all for a good cry to help put the world back in order."

"I need to find some Kleenex," Jessica said.

"Here." Beth snagged a box from a small table, and Jessica took a tissue. "If I may make a suggestion?"

Jessica dabbed at her teary face and looked up. "Go ahead. I need all the help I can get right now." Her mind kept slipping back to the villages she'd been in. Many of the people in them had been kind, and they were just trying to survive. Had they been hurt in the rescue? The thought made her nauseous.

"Why don't you take a hot shower and change into these clothes? I'll get the doctor here, and once you're ready, they can have a look at you. I can stay here with you if you like?"

"Thank you." Jessica gave her a weak smile. "I'd like that. I'm struggling to understand where I am and that I'm safe. I really wasn't sure I'd make it out of this alive."

"You're safe, and you're alive. And after a hot shower and some food, you'll start to feel settled," Beth said gently. "I'll be back shortly."

Jessica went into the bathroom and looked at the pale gray marble tiling and the wonderful array of shower heads in the open shower. Those villagers were washing with buckets of dirty water and using leaves and here, she had a choice of shower heads. Guilt churned her stomach a little more. She found a high-pressure spray, and she allowed herself to relax, breathing deeply and letting the grit slide away. She'd missed hot showers and the warm and sensuous feeling they gave. She wouldn't take them for granted again.

She washed her hair but had to rinse and wash it again to clear the soap remnants. Tears mixed with the shampoo as she kept washing until her hair squeaked beneath her fingers. She climbed out of the shower and looked for the small piece of towel she should use to dry herself off. Instead, she found giant white, fluffy bath towels. She held the towel to her face and cried again. She brushed her hair and decided to dry it properly later; she didn't want to keep Beth waiting too long.

"You look much better, even if my clothing is a little too big on you," Beth said as she put down a book she'd been reading.

"It was such a pleasure to have hot water and big, fluffy towels. But I can't seem to stop crying." Exhaustion suddenly made it hard to stand, and she dropped into a nearby chair.

"You're allowed to cry," Beth said. "The doctor is outside. Shall I bring her in?"

"Yes, please." Jessica looked at her feet and shivered, hoping there were no worms burrowing in them.

Beth left the room, and a small gray-haired woman came in shortly after. "Dr Annabella Short," she said.

"Jessica Landen."

"The commissioner has told me what's happened. Firstly, did you have to deal with any advances of a sexual nature?"

She shuddered. "No, thankfully. I have severe diarrhea, and 'm dehydrated. I think I have a fever, and I'm incredibly tired."

The doctor did a complete examination and took a number of samples. She advised Jessica she didn't need to be hospitalized, but if any of the tests came back positive, that would change, and that she needed to recover for at least three days before considering flying back to London. She gave Jessica instructions about drinking water with added electrolytes, which she left a number of boxes of, and got her to take some loperamide to help deal with her digestive issue.

The doctor also suggested a course of mild sedatives to help her sleep at night, and Jessica promised that if things got worse, she'd seek help. She just hoped that the emotional effects of her time in the village would wear off soon.

Beth came back after the doctor had left. "I've been given strict instructions to ensure you drink plenty of whatever this is." She picked up one of the boxes. "Oral rehydration, blackcurrant flavor," she said as she looked at it. "You've got lemon and orange too."

"I'll start with orange," Jessica said. The doctor's visit was a relief. And it was also yet another reminder of something the tribes' people didn't have access to. She sat beside Beth and picked up her book. "What're you reading?"

"I love detective stories, mysteries, and thrillers. But to be honest, I don't get much time, so I steal a moment here and there. Have you read any Val McDermid?"

"I haven't picked up a book since before my husband died." She'd been overly social during the past couple of years and rarely had time to sit and do anything other than read notes about the next event she was going to. "I always seem to be busy these days. But I think my life is about to change, so maybe I'll start reading again."

There was a knock at the door. Beth answered it and brought a tray into the room. She sat at the dining table with Jessica and uncovered a plate of scrambled eggs, a bowl full of fresh white bread, butter, and strawberry jam. Alongside the food was a mug of cocoa and a mug of coffee.

"The coffee is mine," Beth said. "You shouldn't have any until we've dealt with your dehydration. I thought I'd keep you company while you eat."

Jessica looked at the food before her and nearly wept once again. The past days had been hard with the food different to the sort of food she was used to.

"You just said you thought your life would be changing. How so?" Beth asked. "Has what happened to you caused you to rethink your public service?"

The moment had come for Jessica to put voice to the thoughts she'd had in the villages, and she was certain Beth would be able to help her. "I'd like to have a full debrief with everyone tomorrow, but I'd love to have a run-through with you first if you have the time. Just so I can get my thoughts in order."

"I've blocked out the whole day as I assumed you'd need some support, and I wasn't sure what you'd want from me. So when you've finished eating, we'll get started. In the meantime, tel me about your husband."

Jessica enjoyed her meal and chatted effortlessly to Beth. It was good to talk to someone her age who understood the pressures of life at a level that was a lot more difficult than it appeared to the outside world.

"I've been the American Ambassador to the UK for just over three years," she said, after settling into one of the comfortable armchairs. "I got the job because I'd done a lot of fundraising for the president. She thought I'd do well here and encouraged me to take it after my husband passed. If having a roaring social life is considered doing well, then she was right."

"Yes, this life certainly fills one's calendar, but there's no getting away from the serious side of the job that has to be done at the same time."

Jessica sipped at the cocoa as she pulled the words forward. "I've paid little attention to the serious side, I'm both embarrassed and sorry to say. My staff have written my lines, and I've never really cared about the issues I'm supposed to be representing or backing up."

"Oh, I understand now," Beth said and glanced away.

"I deserve any of your 'stupid, vacuous woman' thoughts. I lived my life according to the social season in London, Paris, and Rome, and dressed accordingly. I have a wide circle of wealthy friends in diplomatic and business circles, and we enjoy meeting up and celebrating."

"It's something we have to do, so I do understand," Beth said. "Tell me how you lost the serious side to the role."

Jessica leaned forward. "I was thinking about that in the villages. While I was at university, I got involved in the YDA movement—'

"YDA?"

"Young Democrats of America." Jessica smiled at the memory. "I did a lot of work around their convention, helping to organize speakers, raising money, and delivering the event itself. I carried on in that kind of work, full of energy and wanting to change America for the better."

"What changed?" Beth asked.

"I got older, more cynical, and found that raising funds for the Democrats over the years meant I completely lost sight of many of the grassroots issues that I wanted to fix. I became jaded." Tears blurred her vision. "The kidnapping brought me up short." Her stomach sank with the thought that she'd spent so much time congratulating herself on the good job she was doing, when in fact, she'd been coasting for years. "I've been taking and not giving. It's terrible. I'm not certain how I've managed to keep out of the political side of the job for so long. I guess I surrounded myself with people who were doing the same."

"It sounds as if you've had a bit of a free ride, if you don't mind me saying. I'm a career civil servant, so I don't think I'd get away with any coasting. But never mind about the past. What about the future?"

She appreciated Beth's honesty, and she was right. The past was done. "Well, that's the thing, I want to go back to being more political. My first task is to figure out what's going on here and then help figure out how to fix it."

"I like that you've an idea for moving forward, but we need to address your safety issue first. I'll timetable the debrief for tomorrow to allow the team some sleep, and I'm sure that Alex will be able to sort your security out. She works for Department 6 in London."

Jessica thought of the beautiful woman who'd appeared out of the darkness. "Is she the team leader?"

"Yes. The American was Mitch Brennan, and she works on the US/Mexico border exposing people-smuggling rings." Beth tilted her head and smiled. "She's a bit of a cowboy, but I like her."

"How did she end up here?"

"As I understand it, she was at a conference in London and was 'borrowed' for this mission," Beth said.

"I was the opening speaker at a conference on crime and security across borders a few days before I came here on holiday." Jessica thought back to the conference and the days of looking forward to her holiday to see the gorillas. "I think I met her briefly." She'd been thinking about her vacation and how she couldn't wait to see the gorillas. She'd paid little attention to the people around her who were doing good work in the world. She looked at Beth. "My kidnappers didn't want a ransom. They took me to their villages to see what our money *hasn't* bought and why our money is needed. But there was a younger section of the villagers who thought that killing me would focus attention on their plight." Jessica ran her hands through her damp hair as she pictured Joseph's rage-filled expression. "The fact that they didn't kill me was due to the argument that the older villagers made. They argued that by showing me village life out in the savannah, I could see what their problems were. They believed I'd do a good job of highlighting their issues. I think...I think today they were going to decide on the next step, whether that meant sending me back to get help or...or killing me to make a statement. I want to help them. We need to figure out where the money is actually going and put a stop to it."

"How are you going to let people know about the problem?"

"I know Toni James; she's an award-winning journalist, and I think this would be right up her street. I'll do a longer press conference to concentrate on the villagers' plight. I think I can get a message out to get things moving again, and I'll certainly lobby for an investigation into where the funding is being used. I was thinking of doing it here, but maybe I'll wait until I'm back in London."

"I'd wait until London. I think you should have a press conference here to show everyone you're safe and uninjured though. I can announce one as soon as you're ready. We'll get you on a flight to London later in the week, when the doctor thinks it's safe for you to leave."

Jessica was about to get her life back. She hoped she had the courage to continue with her new ideas, and that she could return to the ideals she had thirty years ago. Maybe that young idealist was still in there somewhere.

CHAPTER EIGHTEEN

ALEX SAT OPPOSITE MITCH in the dining room and concentrated on her cup of tea, grateful for a moment of quiet to eat her breakfast and reflect on the night. Many people didn't understand that the British officers' mess was silent for breakfast, allowing the officers time to read their paper or just consider their day. She'd never gotten out of the habit, and she loved the silence.

The operation had gone well. There were a few injuries, but nothing more serious that a bullet graze to one soldier's arm. After rescuing the ambassador, the casualty list was the next most important thing. Achieving the objectives with no one seriously injured made her want to dance around the room. Her planning was spot-on, and there was nothing that they hadn't expected—except perhaps the villager having a middle-of-the-night cigarette and pee. Aside from that, everyone had done what they were expected to do, and the op was completed successfully.

Mitch had been the biggest surprise. Her willingness to follow instead of lead showed a level of respect Alex appreciated. It also helped rebuild some of the trust she'd lost in Mitch after the initial failed op.

"What are you thinking about?" Mitch asked. "You looked so serious and thoughtful, and then you smiled and your whole face changed. Penny for your thoughts?"

"Interestingly, it was about you," Alex said.

"Just what I like to hear. You were remembering the time in London when we first met, I expect," Mitch said and gave her a wicked grin. "There was a lot about that night to remember, and I've enjoyed the memory every night since," she whispered. "I still want you back in my bed. Today would be perfect. I'll follow you up if you want to go now."

Alex giggled. "As strange as it may seem, I was remembering how you followed command last night. There was no bed, I'm afraid."

"I wanted to impress you so that you understood I can learn. It was a good op, wasn't it?" Mitch's expression turned serious.

"Yes, it was. We've been lucky with the team you assembled down here too. I assume the right US government department will compensate them," Alex said.

Mitch chuckled. "Because you have no idea who might pay or where the money will come from?"

The blush rose on Alex's cheeks. "It's not like I should know it, is it? You don't know who pays my budget either, so we're quits."

"And then we disappear into the dark world of departments that may or may not exist, and projects that are being funded by someone somewhere, not always with the knowledge of those supposedly in charge." Mitch grinned and wiggled her eyebrows. "It's what makes this all so exciting. We're doing an essential job that the majority of the population don't want to know about for whatever reason. But we're making a difference."

Alex nodded, though she didn't want to get into a deep discussion about the black ops world. Today wasn't the sort of day for that conversation. "I expect we won't get much out of the ambassador until tomorrow. We should get the latest info and make sure that my prime minister and your president are both up to date."

Mitch shook her head and smiled. "Not up for a philosophical tangle today? Maybe you'd be interested in a physical one then. You didn't respond to my offer."

Alex rolled her eyes. "If you play your cards right, we might have the afternoon and evening off, and we can see." Alex's body responded in the way Mitch's presence seemed to demand, as Mitch grinned and looked her over, the offer clear in her eyes.

Issues remained between them though. Should she really just set them aside like they didn't matter for a night of passion?

They walked to the high commissioner's office and were apprised of the ambassador's current health. The assistant asked them to wait because the commissioner wanted a quick word.

"Hello," Beth said. "Well done last night. The ambassador is back safe and sound and should be much better by tomorrow. I am spending some time with her today. We'll debrief her at eleven a.m. tomorrow. Perhaps you can debrief your teams before that."

"Certainly, ma'am," Alex said.

Beth closed the door of her assistant's office. "In order to keep the ambassador safe we'd like to keep security on her from the moment she leaves this building until she's safely on the plane. Can you liaise with the security team to make sure this happens, please? Although we doubt anyone would attempt anything now that she's been rescued, we'd like to play things as safely as possible."

Alex nodded. It made sense, if only so the ambassador felt safe.

"We also have a slight issue. I suggested that an agent from Department 6 be on her team of bodyguards, but she wants you, Lieutenant Brennan. She said she needed someone she knew could look after her."

"No." Mitch's eyes flashed. "I'm an operational officer who works on the ground. I don't have a Secret Service background, I have no idea how to talk to ambassadors, and spending hours standing in corridors would drive me insane. Besides, if she wants a bodyguard, she only has to make a request to the embassy, and they'll provide one. Full or part time."

"Right," Beth said. "Is there any way she can convince you to take the job?"

"No." Mitch crossed her arms "Nothing will convince me. I'll debrief in London and then head back to Texas. I need to get back to my normal life."

Alex's stomach dropped. She'd hoped to have a little more time than that, but it was clear Mitch wasn't about to slow down, and definitely not for a woman she barely knew. They hadn't had enough time to see if their initial attraction was worth exploring, and it didn't look like they were going to. She thought back to her conversation with her friends before she left. She wanted a real partner, not someone who galivanted around the world she same way she did. She wanted someone steady who could give her their whole heart. That wasn't Mitch. Still, it stung.

"Bodyguard. What is she thinking?" Mitch muttered as they walked to the security office.

"I'd be chuffed to bits if she wanted me as a bodyguard for a few months. Mind you, I'd like to think I could come back and do the job I have now." Alex only wanted Mitch to take the position so they'd have time together.

Mitch's laugh had a humorless edge. "Yeah, right. Like I'd want to spend three months bored out of my head for a promotion to captain that I could get just by going home and doing my job. I can see my soldiers in Texas being impressed with their boss getting promoted for being a stuffed shirt. It'll look so impressive on my jacket too. Bribed by an ambassador for looking after her in her fancy house."

"I just thought—"

"I don't want anything to do with it. I'm going back to my room to calm down. I'll let you sort out security. See you later."

She walked away, leaving Alex wishing she could say that she wanted Mitch to be a bodyguard and stay in London so they could explore the magnetism between them. But that wasn't fair to Mitch, was it? It wasn't part of who she was, and it was wrong to want her to change just so they could be together for what would probably be a short amount of time anyway.

She organized the security although she was sure her security team were on the ball. They raised the terrorist level to orange and put someone in the corridor outside the ambassador's room. Alex was satisfied that all was in order.

She sat in the shade on the patio behind the Commission with a bottle of water and looked out over the shrub garden. Most of the grounds were red, sandy soil and trees, but there were a few sculptured plants breaking it up. She had a bit of thinking to do. Somehow, Mitch had gotten under her skin, and she hated the thought of losing her. Being with her the last few days in a working environment had only added to that feeling. Mitch was infuriating, quick to change things, always taking risks...and Alex wanted more. More time with her, more time with her body, more time for sex. More time to get to know the tender, vulnerable side that she kept so well hidden.

The next couple of days would be their last. But two days wouldn't cut it. She needed more. She'd always been looking for a relationship that was longer than a one-night sex-fest, but that looked like it was off the cards. She should probably just accept that she was only likely to get a couple of nights with Mitch, followed by the pain of her leaving. Or she could stop now and have the memory of their one glorious night together, a thought to keep her warm in the cold of winter.

The thing was, she was already upset. She didn't want them to be apart, and there was no way this could resolve other than monthly commutes or something similar. Could she be happy with that? *No.* That kind of relationship wasn't what she was looking for. If she was honest, she thought that Mitch might simply return to her old life. It would be so easy for her to continue her past behavior. Perhaps Alex should consider going to America and finding work there instead. She had no idea whether she'd find a job there though. She was career Army and Special Ops; she knew little else. And really, she didn't want to leave the UK.

If neither of them was willing to sacrifice for the other, then maybe they simply weren't meant to be more than they'd been. The thought made her ache inside.

Alex found herself knocking on Mitch's door, as if her thoughts had taken her there on autopilot. Her emotions were riotous, and this probably wasn't a good idea. But damn it if she wasn't determined to spend whatever time she could with Mitch before it all fell apart.

"Hey," Mitch said and opened the door wider for Alex to come in.

"I wondered how you were?" She smiled and followed Mitch into the room.

"You mean after you criticized me for not wanting a boring job with the suits and being negative about it?" Mitch crossed her arms.

"I'm sorry. That wasn't my intention. Please believe me," Alex said. "I was trying to get you to think about staying in London for a few months so that we could be together. I made it sound all wrong...that you should take a job you didn't want for the promotion. I wanted you to take it to be with me." Alex swallowed hard and tried not to break eye contact.

Mitch didn't move a muscle. Her expression was still stony, and it wasn't clear whether she'd even heard what Alex said.

"I'm sorry." Alex finally looked away. "I thought what we have might be worth fighting for. I'll leave and save embarrassing myself any further." She turned for the door, thinking that Mitch might stop her, but there was nothing but silence, so she left and crossed the corridor to her own room. She curled up on her side, tears sliding down her cheeks. If this was the agony of being without Mitch when they'd spent so little time together, perhaps it was good it was over now. It would've only hurt even more when it blew to bits later, right?

CHAPTER NINETEEN

MITCH HADN'T MOVED SINCE Alex had left her room some time ago. She couldn't decide what her emotions were or what they were telling her. She *was* certain that she'd messed up a relationship with the one decent woman she'd ever had in her life. She'd hurt Alex, and when she'd said they had something to explore, Mitch froze like a deer in headlights, unable to think of a response.

She'd never expected to feel like this. *Think instead of act. How am I feeling?*

Scared. She was scared, and she rarely felt fear outside of work. Work fear, she could handle. Without it, she'd be too hasty with her own and other peoples' lives. That fear was good and made sense.

This unease was something else. It had the same symptoms: the nausea, the adrenaline pumping around her body, and the heightened awareness. The thought of losing Alex gave her all these feelings and more. Leaving her would mean a separation from something Mitch wanted and needed to keep her happy and to feel...loved? How did other people cope? She'd read about love and how it affected people, but she'd never had it. Never even come close and had thought she was incapable of it.

Maybe she should talk to her momma. She looked at the clock and thought she'd get her before she began her day. She smiled at the thought of Momma sitting on her back porch with a mug of coffee and her iPad, beginning her day quietly. This would interrupt her peace and quiet, that was for sure. She video-called anyway.

"Hey, Momma, how're you?" Mitch asked. "I can see you're in your usual spot, so the weather must be good."

"Mitch! What a lovely surprise. When you said you were on an operation, I didn't expect to hear from you for a while."

"The operation is over, and it was successful...so it could mean I'll be back in the US soon."

"That sounds good. I'm glad you're okay." Momma smiled and raised her eyebrow. "So what's with the hesitation about coming back home? You finally meet a woman that lasted more than one night?"

She constantly teased Mitch about her inability to settle. She cleared her throat. "Yeah, well, I need some advice."

"You're asking my advice about a woman? Sweetie, you know I've forgotten anything I ever knew about the dating game."

Mitch knew full well that wasn't true. "I think if I haven't already lost her, I might, if I don't say and do the right thing. But what the hell is the right thing?"

"Start at the beginning, tell me about her. Where did you meet?"

Mitch gave her the rundown, from their meeting at the club in London to working together on the op in Africa. She even told her about the fuck-up she'd made and how Alex had covered for her instead of sending her packing. "She's smart, sexy as hell, kind, and she keeps me on my toes." She sighed and closed her eyes. "She's in my dreams and damn near all I think about when I'm not in the middle of a gunfight."

"She sounds special. Go on."

"I've been offered a job as a bodyguard to the American Ambassador to London for a few months," Mitch said, "and I'm likely to get my promotion, whether it's for the op or for doing this job. I assume I'd go back to my regular work in a new position after the bodyguard thing was over."

"Wow, and you'll get a promotion too. But do you want this job?" Momma asked. "You've always wanted to be out in the world playing secret agent."

Mitch gave her momma an honest account of her reaction to the job offer.

"And did it end there?" Momma asked.

Mitch relayed the story of Alex's appearance in her room, then drew in a deep breath. "And here I am."

"You didn't say *anything*?" Momma said.

"I didn't. I know I should've said something, but I couldn't think of a single fucking thing to say. So she left."

"Firstly, I think you need to work out what you want and how much you want it." Momma said. "Once you've done that, you can work out how you're going to make that happen. So what do you want?"

Mitch flopped back on the bed and stared at the ceiling. She answered from her heart instead of her head. "Alex. Since she walked out of this room, I've realized how much I want her, how much I want to see where this goes."

"How much *do* you want her? That's the question that you'll struggle to answer, but be honest. Do you want her enough to travel once a month to England for two days with her, or once every two months if she comes to you? Do you want her enough to not be with anyone else?"

Mitch considered the question. "Yeah, I'd do that. It'd be damn hard, and I'm sure that our jobs would interfere with the timings, so we'd have lots of problems." Between them, there could be months of missed calls and texts, let alone visits.

"Could or would Alex come out to the US?" Momma asked.

"I suspect that's an option later, but she has her own home, and she would only come if we were committed to each other. It's too soon to think about that."

"So could or would you stay in the UK?"

Mitch sighed and rubbed her face. "And we're back to being the ambassador's bodyguard. That would keep me there for a while and would mean I got to spend time with Alex, and we could explore what we have together."

"So now that you've thought it through calmly and worked out the possibilities, what's your next step?" Momma asked, her tone suggesting she already knew the answer.

If she was at home, she'd invite Alex somewhere romantic, show her what she had to offer, and hope it was enough. She could wait until they got back to London, but that was days away, and in the meantime, she needed to show Alex that she needed her. But what could she do in Solunwa? There was nothing she could think of that would romance Alex. Maybe Neela could help.

"I know what I've got to do, thank you." Mitch smiled and touched her momma's face on the screen. "I'm off to organize a romantic evening somewhere in the middle of a big city and see if I can woo her. I don't know what I'd do without you. You always help me get out of my head. I don't tell you enough that I love you."

"I love you too. Now go and get your girl. Let me know how it turns out."

Mitch hurried along to the intelligence office to speak to Neela to see if she knew anyone in her contacts who could help Mitch organize her romantic plans. When Mitch said she wanted something with wildlife if that were possible, Neela knew exactly what she could do, and a phone call later, it was set.

Mitch went back upstairs to Alex's room. The time had come to fix things between them, and she only hoped that she wasn't too late.

CHAPTER TWENTY

ALEX OPENED HER EYES at the knocking, trying to gain a sense of place and time. The memory of her conversation with Mitch and her feeling of sorrow came flooding back like a wave, drowning all other thoughts. The knocking started again.

"Alex, are you in there? It's Mitch."

"Go away. I don't want to talk," Alex called out. The last thing she needed was Mitch coming to explain why things wouldn't work between them.

"I know you don't. If I was you, I wouldn't want to talk to me either. But this is important, and if you don't let me in, I'll say what I need to out here. I hope it's okay for everyone to know our business."

Alex got up and threw the door open. "Come in." No doubt her hair was a mess, and her face would be full of sleep creases from her bedcover. Not exactly the look of a woman who was in control and ready to face romantic rejection. "Let me go and freshen up so that we can talk."

When she came back from the bathroom, Mitch was pacing the room like a caged animal.

"Please sit," Mitch said.

She looked so serious that Alex was worried about what she was going to say. She wasn't sure she'd be able to cope with more heartbreak.

"When you came to my room, I froze. That's not me. I can always be relied on to bust through things like a bull in a china shop. But I froze, and I couldn't think straight. I took in what you said, but I couldn't say anything... Then it felt like you were pulling away from me, and I didn't know how to stop it."

"Yes, well–"

"No, let me say this. This thing between us... I mean, it hasn't been easy, has it? But I can't stop thinking about you. I want to see where this will go too. But I've never done anything like this before, and part of my freezing was the thought of us having a longer relationship. And when I analyzed my fear, I realized I was more afraid of losing you than I was of having a relationship with you. I need you; you're the calm in my constant storm, and somehow, you get me. You make me think about things I've never cared about before and if you aren't with me, I worry about how empty my life will feel and how reckless I'll be because I won't have you to come home to."

Mitch put her hands on her hips as if she were almost daring Alex to make fun of her. She practically bled vulnerability, and there was no mistaking the fear in her eyes. Alex's breath came out in a rush. "I just cried myself to sleep. I thought that we were finished, that you didn't want to spend more time with me, and had nothing to say except you wanted to go home. I had no idea that you felt so much, but it still hasn't resolved the biggest of our problems. How can we spend time together?" She was ragged inside, but Mitch's words were a balm she had only hoped for.

"I'm really sorry, Alex." Mitch ran her hands through her hair. "For being a jerk, for not knowing what to say...for not seeing how damn special you are right from the beginning."

"Your apology is accepted. Come here, and let's see if we can sort this out." Alex waited until Mitch sat and put her arms around her. She kissed her, slow and deep, hoping that all her feelings were clear on her lips.

They parted, and Alex took a breath. Mitch, too, looked a little shaken.

"I've already done some thinking. I rang my momma and asked her advice," Mitch said. "It came down to knowing what I want, which is you, and that to have you, I need to take that ambassador job, so we get the time to create something special."

"But you don't want to do that job. What you said about stuffed shirts made me think of Action Man playing Barbie. It's just not you." The thought of Mitch volunteering to calm her raging bull for three months was certainly something she hadn't expected.

Mitch shrugged. "It was either do that or try long distance, and that just isn't going to work, not when we're just finding our feet together. You can bet my ops will be happening on a different timescale to yours, and we could go three months between visits, which can probably only last a few days. No, let's do this. It gives us time to work things out together."

Alex's heart swelled at Mitch's gesture. "Are you sure?"

"Yes, very sure. Let me show you." Mitch leaned in, her lips meeting Alex's, and this time the kiss held promises of far more than just a little romance.

"It's an incredible sacrifice," Alex said. "You need to tell me if you can't do it, and we'll talk it through. Please be honest with me. I don't want to wake up one day and find you've buggered off back to America without letting us work out possible alternatives."

"I promise. Let's seal it with a kiss."

Alex wanted more than just a kiss but surrendered to Mitch's plea and melted into it. She wanted more, but Mitch was already pulling away.

"I need to go tell the ambassador I'll take the position. I have something planned for us this afternoon. Pack a bag for one night with your best evening wear and wear casual clothes for the trip. I'll pick you up in forty-five minutes."

"What? Where are we going?" This spontaneity was something she could get used to. Eventually.

"It's a surprise. I want to romance you properly so that you remember Africa and our time here together." Mitch grimaced. "Not the bad stuff, obviously." She shook her head and grinned. "You're wasting time. I'll be back here in forty-three minutes."

She kissed Alex gently and left the room. Alex sighed. Life with Mitch was likely to be a fairground ride. An hour or two ago, she'd been at rock bottom, but Mitch had managed to pull her up and finally given her something to look forward to. Mitch the romantic was something she'd like to see. And Mitch the girlfriend... Well, that was going to be quite the adventure.

* * *

A giraffe stuck its head through the open window with its long, raspy tongue extended and took the banana from Alex's hand, making her giggle like a child. A baby giraffe watched from below, too small to reach the hotel room window.

Mitch had managed to get them bed and breakfast at a luxury hotel that had giraffes who popped in for snacks from guests more than willing to hand over their food. The late afternoon light pooled across the lawns between the tall slim trees and added a sparkle to the magic.

Their room had a king-sized bed, front and center, and a balcony with a table and chairs. Alex chuckled. She'd noticed the bed but not much else. She made herself take in the room, so she'd always remember this moment. It was decorated in deep red, browns, and dark orange, which gave it a strong earthy feel. It had a sofa that looked comfortable, with a high back and soft cushions, although Alex was giggling again about when they'd have time to use it as was intended. "I feel like a child being given her most precious dreams. I don't know how you managed this, but I'm so thankful that you did."

"Is that your inner child having fun?" Mitch asked from where she leaned over the windowsill, looking out at the savannah.

"Er, no." Heat rose in her cheeks. "I was thinking about how I noticed the bed and not much else when we came into the room. Then I wondered whether we'd ever manage to sit on that sofa, and my mind went all over the place."

"It's good to know you haven't stopped wanting me for my body." Mitch gently took Alex's hand and pulled her close. "We've got afternoon tea with the giraffes in a minute, and dinner is at seven thirty. So we don't have time to try out the bed," she said between soft kisses.

"You mean I'l have to wait until after dinner? How am I supposed to manage that?" During the op, Alex had thought of Mitch constantly. She'd thought about the sex, sure, and she thought she could wait until they were both free of responsibilities. But now, the handsome parcel that was Mitch Brennan stood before her, waiting to be unwrapped and just like at Christmas, she didn't want to wait.

"I promise it'll be worth it. Come on, we can't miss this."

The shower wasn't as fast as it should have been, despite their attempts to get ready separately. Quick touches led to slow kisses, and Mitch walked Alex back toward the bed at one point, only to be interrupted by the passing shadow of a giraffe.

A typically English high tea was already being served by the time they made it to the dining room. There were china bowls full of cream, strawberry jam, honey, and plates of butter sitting beside enormous scones. "I won't have more than one. Otherwise I'll be too full and too relaxed for other activities later." She winked at Mitch and got a wicked grin in response. "You know, we could be in England with the way this is set up. It's perfect."

"I'm enjoying the view, for sure," Mitch said.

"Me too," Alex said, looking out the window and over the lawn.

"I was looking at a different view." Mitch stared at her across the table and put her hand over Alex's. "And now you're going to tell me how to eat this scone, so I don't make some kind of ignorant American mistake." She took one from the pile and put it on her plate. "What's next?"

"First things first, you either break the scone open across the middle or slice it with your knife," Alex said. "I tend to use a knife because I don't want to be too messy, and whenever I try to open them with my hands, they crumble to pieces. Then you either spread jam on one side of the scone and put cream on top, or cream on the bottom and jam on top. I'm a jam on the bottom, cream on top kind of gal." Heat rushed up her neck at the unintended, but accurate, innuendo.

"I thought you might be. We could take this back to the hotel room and explore the best places for the cream and jam and which way around we prefer them."

Mitch's eyes danced, and the sensuality in her gaze caused Alex's body to take another leap in the lust stakes. She'd never last until later tonight. There was a chance she might spontaneously combust right now. Alex cut her scone open and put jam and cream on half before tucking in. "You'll have to teach me some American food traditions one day," she said, hoping she wasn't being too presumptuous.

"Thanksgiving is *the* thing. We could spend it with Momma and help her cook up a storm with turkey, green bean casserole, and pumpkin pie." Mitch's eyes watered slightly, and she looked away, her jaw clenching.

"What's wrong?"

"I miss being home for the first time in ten years. Being with you is making me feel and think strange things," Mitch said. "What have you done to me?"

A staff manager came to their table before Alex could respond. "The staff will clear away the afternoon crockery, and we can go outside. There are small jars of molasses snacks for you to give to the giraffes."

Mitch's mood seemed to shift with the wind, and she grinned, all traces of sadness gone. "Let's go."

Outside the hotel, the giraffes approached, looking for the expected snacks in their hands. The guests were supervised, because they'd been told that though the giraffes may look adorable, a headbutt from one in play was enough to smash in a person's face. Alex struggled to believe there was a difficult bone in a giraffe's body, and the whole experience left her beyond words. The giant creatures took the sweet gently from her hands, and interacting with their majestic bodies gave her goosebumps. Mitch put her arm around Alex's shoulders, and she leaned into her, loving the strength and solidity. When the snacks were gone, the giraffes headed off to their nighttime haunts, and the thirty or so guests made their way indoors.

They held hands as they headed back to their room, a feeling of anticipation rising with every step. "That has got to be the most perfect thing in my life so far." Alex flopped onto the bed and stared at the ceiling.

Mitch put her hand to her chest, and her eyes widened. "You mean our night together earlier this month *wasn't* the most perfect thing?"

"Well, it comes close, but I never expected to be feeding giraffes in Africa with my ...my..." She stopped, at a loss and unable to take the words back. She shrugged and moved on. "And we can make things even more perfect later."

"I love being called yours." Mitch jumped onto the bed and kissed her.

There was nothing gentle about it, and Alex responded, pressing her body hard to Mitch's.

Mitch pulled away, breathing hard. "Once we start this, I'm not going to stop until you've passed out from pleasure." She stood and pulled her clothes off, lingering a little when Alex propped herself up to watch. 'I'm going to shower and clean up. Know that if you join me, we'll definitely miss dinner."

"I don't want to miss anything, so you're on your own." Alex somehow managed to stay on the bed despite also being desperate to join Mitch. She was enjoying getting to know the side of Mitch that she'd had glimpses of in London. She was thoughtful, kind, generous, and so much more than just a hothead with a gun. The bull in the china shop was still in there, but she was becoming more measured. Alex herself was also changing, and she thought about that a little. She'd taken charge of the operation and done well even with the US contingent. She was happy with how it had gone, and hopefully the debrief tomorrow would echo that. She'd done what she needed to do to prove herself and found someone special to have in her life at the same time.

Mitch came out of the bathroom wrapped in a thick brown towel. "All yours, beautiful."

Alex luxuriated in the shower and washed her hair. She wanted to look perfect tonight, for their first night together as something more than a one-night stand. She came out of the shower with a towel around her body and another around her hair.

Mitch's eyes darkened with desire as she looked Alex over. "I thought we could get dressed together so that you wouldn't be wandering around in front of me naked and feeling self-conscious. Or think that I was watching your every move, which I would have been. Obviously." She stood up and dropped the towel to the floor. "And I wouldn't have to torture myself watching you get dressed because I'll be trying to look my best too."

Alex's knees went weak, and she nearly sank down onto them right there and then. She was dying to rediscover Mitch's muscular body, sculpted from the physicality of her job and her desire to stay in fighting shape. And there were a couple scars and a few tattoos that Alex would definitely be exploring in depth later.

Mitch tugged at the towel around Alex, and she let it slide off slowly. Then she pulled off the one on her head and let her wet hair fall around her shoulders. Mitch gulped like she'd been struck breathless. Alex took a few steps back and gave her a teasing smile. "It's a good plan. I'm sure we won't find it distracting at all to be fully naked together."

Just before seven, they were ready to go to the courtyard for cocktails, with Alex in the same lightweight dress she'd worn to visit the president. She would have liked to dress up more, but it wasn't like she'd brought anything fancy with her on the mission. There was no one else there when they arrived, and they were served by a waiter once they were seated. Mitch ordered an old fashioned, and Alex decided to try a John Collins, and they sat in the evening sunshine watching some warthogs only a few feet away, rufling around in the undergrowth looking for leftover molasses treats from the giraffes.

"I didn't expect to be sitting here this evening, with or without you," Alex said. "Some days start out awful and everything you dread happens, and before you know it, it all changes and the sun comes out and wipes away the shadows you had before sunrise. I know I keep saying it but thank you for this."

Mitch kissed Alex's knuckles. "Thank you for giving me enough chances to finally get my head out of my ass."

They ate an exquisite dinner and lingered over coffee with a Talisker scotch on the side. Alex thought she'd gone to heaven. "Nearly every conversation with you is a surprise. You enjoy poetry—not expected; Marvel Movies— expected; and classical music—not expected." She took the last sip of her scotch.

Mitch tilted her head slightly. "I could say the same thing. I knew you worked in Africa and did a lot of work playing the ditzy blond, but I didn't realize that you speak five languages. I speak American and passable Spanish, which I learned on the job. I'm so glad you like spicy food. I thought all Brits loved it bland."

"Shall we head upstairs to see what other surprises we can unwrap?" Alex simply couldn't wait another second.

"God, yes," Mitch said. "Lead on, darlin'."

Alex headed up the wide wooden staircase, and Mitch put her arm around her waist. As Mitch unlocked the door, Alex took the opportunity to get a little closer and kissed Mitch's neck.

"I'm going to take forever to do this. I can't concentrate," Mitch said as she inserted the keycard for the third time.

The door finally swung open and banged against the wall. Mitch kissed her hard and slid her hands under Alex's dress to cup her butt cheeks. She lifted her up, and Alex wrapped her legs around Mitch's waist. She continued to nuzzle Mitch's neck, kissing and nipping at the sensitive skin as Mitch kicked the room door closed behind them. Mitch placed her gently onto the bed, her eyes dark with desire.

"I'd like to undress you," Mitch said.

Alex looked into eyes that stared back with such strength, and she thought they could see into her soul. "I'm all yours," she said. "I want to strip you naked too."

"Have at it," Mitch said huskily as she stepped back, pulling Alex to her feet.

Their mouths met, and the kiss was so full and long it left Alex breathless. She'd imagined this moment all day and now it was here, she wanted to take her time and give Mitch all of her. Mitch turned her around and undid the black necklace, kissing her before she placed it gently on the dresser.

Before Alex could move again, Mitch was behind her, undoing her dress zipper. It slid down much too slowly as Mitch kissed her bare skin as the dress fell. It was sweet torture, and Alex could barely wait until they were naked. Once she was down to her underwear, Mitch moved around to face her, and she lightly grazed her fingers over the curve of Alex's breasts.

"Did you know red is my favorite color?" Mitch asked as she slid her fingertips beneath a bra strap.

"I'm glad you like it. But you should stand so I can catch up," Alex said. She took off Mitch's tie and put it with her necklace, liking the symbolism. The vest followed quickly. She undid the buttons on Mitch's shirt and slowly drew it open, kissing her bare chest. Alex stood back to look at the tempting sight of Mitch's small, perfect breasts peeking out of her shirt. She slid the shirt off and sighed. Mitch put her arms around her and this time, the kiss was gentle, unhurried. Alex couldn't get enough.

She got to her knees and undid the belt and catch at the top of Mitch's pants. Mitch drew in her breath as she pulled the pants down and kissed her bare thighs. She kissed her way up Mitch's legs and took a moment to visit the wet patch on the boxers with her lips. Mitch took off the rest of her clothes and tossed it all aside.

Mitch pulled Alex into her arms. "You're so fucking beautiful."

She kissed Alex gently and let her go to remove her bra. A moment later, Mitch wrapped her hands around each breast and kissed Alex's nipples. She lost herself in the feeling of pure lust that ripped through her. She removed her panties, and they dropped onto the bed.

Alex kissed Mitch on the lips as she ran her hands up Mitch's stomach and onto her breasts.

Mitch sucked in a sharp breath. "There's another bit of my body that's crying out for you."

Mitch opened her legs, and as Alex moved down her abdomen to the curls between her legs, she could smell Mitch's need, a warm earthy smell that heightened Alex's.

She slid her tongue along Mitch's length, and Mitch pushed her hips into the air. Alex pressed her hand against Mitch's stomach and pushed her back down. She wasn't anywhere near as strong as Mitch, but she could easily take control.

Alex concentrated her efforts and found those areas that had Mitch reacting the most, and she sucked and licked her way around her. She looked at Mitch, and their eyes met.

Mitch's eyes half-lidded. "Don't stop," she whispered.

Alex didn't reply, and she had no intention of stopping. She smiled wickedly and slipped two fingers inside her. She put in a third finger and worked up a gentle rhythm. Mitch moved in time with her, breathing heavily, but she never took her eyes off Alex. Every move within her increased Mitch's breathing, and Alex felt her heart beating more quickly. Mitch spasmed, and her whole body went rigid for a moment, before she tensed around Alex's fingers and collapsed against the bed. Mitch pulled Alex up the length of her body, and Alex withdrew from the warmth and the heavy muscles that had held her fingers. She lay her head on Mitch's breast and put an arm across her chest.

They lay like that, silent and close for some time. Mitch's heartbeat slowed, and her breathing evened out.

"I hope you're not falling asleep," Mitch said softly, her fingers trailing along Alex's back. "It's my turn."

Alex sighed deeply at how good it felt to have Mitch's weight on top of her, and as Mitch explored her body until she begged for release, she really didn't think life could get any better.

CHAPTER TWENTY-ONE

THE UNEXPECTED BREAK HAD been something that Mitch would never forget. Time away from the operation and the High Commission had given them both breathing space and the opportunity to be alone together, to get to know each other far better. Now she was sure they had something special, and they needed to allow t to grow. Mitch didn't want to walk away from those feelings or throw away the one chance she might have to find her soulmate.

She was damaged goods in some respects. She'd gotten lucky with her momma and had loved her almost since they first met at the vending machine, so she understood she could love, if on y to a small degree. But she'd never managed to find the person that she wanted to spend time with.

"Are you happy to do the debrief, Mitch?" Alex asked.

Alex was trusting her to take a responsible position, which was something she had to practice if she was going to take a more senior role, and her adrenaline popped. "Yeah, please. I'd love the practice."

The US Ambassador came into the room followed by the British High Commissioner. Alex hit the record button on the machine in the middle of the table.

"I asked the high commissioner to be present for my debrief; she knows much of the story anyway, and I need someone at my side," the ambassador said.

"Are you happy to be here and support the ambassador, ma'am?" Mitch asked.

"Of course, I've been supporting her since she arrived and am happy to continue to do so," the commissioner said.

"Ma'am," Mitch said to the ambassador. "The purpose of having this debrief is to get a full record, in your own words, of what happened to you. It will never be made public, but we have to understand what happened and how to avoid it happening again in the future."

"Yes, I fully understand that, and it will be good to get things off my chest too. I need some assurances though. Who *will* hear the debrief record?"

Mitch turned to Alex, her eyebrows raised. "I think this is your answer."

"We would submit it to General Moss in Department 6, and he would forward it through to whomever he considered necessary in your embassy," Alex said. "Is that a problem?"

The ambassador nodded. "If I give details of what happened, such as the names of people or villages, and any of it finds its way to the president, government, or armed forces of Minabo, the villagers who kidnapped me will be killed or forcibly removed from their homes. I'm hoping to counter that with some investigative reporting and film and photographs of the villages. But I need time to set that in motion."

"I understand," Alex said. "You believe that once your news reports are out there, it won't matter. But it needs to be kept under wraps until then. We can discuss with the general how we should proceed once we have the information from you. I suspect that he'll lose it in his office for a few weeks. But don't tell anyone I said that."

"Perhaps we should start at the beginning. Can you tell us how you came to be in Minabo, ma'am," Mitch asked.

Jessica told them about how she'd decided to make the trip, and why she'd decided to take it alone.

"The kidnapping must have been terrifying. Tell us exactly what happened, as you remember it," Mitch said.

Jessica related what she could recall about the kidnapping and her horror when one of the men killed the driver. "I want to protect the villagers, but I don't want to protect the three young men who kidnapped me. The one who murdered Jono is Joseph Bitalo. His father, Mukasa Bitalo, is the man behind my kidnapping, and he was shocked when he discovered that his son had killed the driver for no reason." She began to cry but managed to cont nue to talk. "They could have left him tied up, and it would have made little difference; he wasn't known to anyone in the villages, so he couldn't have pointed anyone in that direction."

"Do you want to continue, ma'am?" Mitch asked. "We can stop for a break."

"No, I just want to get this over with." Jessica briefly closed her eyes. "It's one step toward getting my life back."

Jessica described her first couple of days in the village and the kindness of Lulu the chief's wife. "The first village was like Millionaire's Row compared to some of the other villages we went to. Those other villages had virtually nothing. Their water came from miles away, many of them collected in containers by the women who walked back and forth daily. The lucky villages had a school within five miles, and the children walked there and back. Most had no shoes. The hygiene in these villages was poor, and so was their health. Many didn't have malaria nets and death was common. Their life was hard." She wiped away tears. "It was heartbreaking."

"How did you get to the villages you visited?" Mitch asked.

"On foot, mostly. I had a lift in the back of a truck somewhere near the end because my feet were sore, and I was struggling to walk. The women said my soles needed hardening up. They gave me moccasin slippers, which were better than the sliders that most women seemed to wear."

The ambassador recounted the story about the final vi lage from where she was rescued and the meeting between the elders of the tribes and how they had managed to talk down the young hotheads who thought that violence was the answer.

"Here's the thing that we need to deal with," Jessica said, her voice hardening. "Millions of dollars are being sent here to aid these people, but there's a dam somewhere, and it isn't flowing beyond a few greedy people. I'm going to start turning over rocks and making some noise, and I'll keep doing so until we get answers. I imagine I'm going to become rather unpopular."

Mitch looked at the ambassador and could see that she was flagging. "I think we should finish there, ma'am. I think we have all the information apart from a few names and places we can fill in later."

Alex nodded. "I've nothing to add. Thanks, Lieutenant Brennan."

"Lieutenant Brennan, perhaps we can meet around four to discuss your role when you come to work for me," the ambassador said. "I'd like to talk about what you hope for and what I'm looking for."

Mitch nodded. "Yes, ma'am."

The ambassador and the commissioner left the room. Mitch switched the recorder off and turned to Alex. "Damn. She must've been so fucking scared."

Alex shook her head. "And knowing that the children she spent time with are likely to have a short lifespan? It must have been emotionally exhausting."

They headed for lunch and talked about the logistics of heading home. Mitch made a few calls to her bosses to let them know their ETA in London.

Mitch knocked on the door to the ambassador's suite at exactly 1600 hours, with pen and paper in hand, and it was promptly opened by the commissioner.

"I'm going to my office. Perhaps you'll let me know when you've finished and whether the ambassador needs me to come back?" she asked.

"Of course, ma'am," Mitch said.

The ambassador sat in an armchair wearing flowery lounge pants and a striped shirt. "I'm sorry about the strange clothes. They haven't found all my luggage yet, so I'm wearing the commissioner's spare clothes...and beggars can't be choosers." She smoothed down the shirt self-consciously.

"They look quite colorful, ma'am, but not that bad," Mitch said, thinking that Alex would have known just what to say.

"Let me stand up, and you'll get a better idea," the ambassador said.

"Ah, I get it now." Mitch tried to keep a straight face at the sight of her new boss wearing pants that were too big around the waist and hips and way too short in the legs. The shirt was too large and clashed horribly with the pants. "If you give me the job, will I get to see this sort of fashion every day?" She grinned and hoped the ambassador had a sense of humor.

The ambassador's eyes flashed, and she grimaced as she sat back down. "I have fantastic fashion sense, *actually*."

Maybe she'd overstepped after all. "I already know that, ma'am. I saw you at the conference in London when you gave the opening speech, and you looked like a million bucks."

"Good save, lieutenant," the ambassador said and gave her a wry smile. "So take a seat. Let's see what you think I'm looking for, and I can tell you what I'm actually looking for. And then we can see what we need to do to make it happen."

Mitch took a deep breath. "I have no idea what you might need, ma'am. I thought your security was likely to be top notch and involve US agencies. As you know, I normally work out on the ground with a team. This would be something completely out of my wheelhouse. However, I figure you're looking for someone who can accompany you to your engagements, be visible, and keep you safe while you turn over these stones and search out snakes. I can certainly do that."

"That's it exactly. I'll obviously need a team, but I'll want you to lead it. I want someone I can trust, Mitch, and right now, that's you. Can you do that?"

"Ma'am, of course I can. I may need a little brush-up on some diplomacy skills, but I can do that in your downtime or when it's convenient for you to have someone else guard you." Mitch would need a quick course on etiquette as much as anything. Alex would be her go-to.

"Call me Jessica when we're in private, please. When I asked Alex if she could recommend you for the role, she gave you a good report. She did say that you were expecting to be made captain when you returned to the US."

"I was hoping that would be the case," Mitch said.

"I want you with me as a captain, so I'll ask the embassy to make that happen," Jessica said. "I'd prefer you as a major, because I think you deserve it, and the extra rank will give you status, but I suspect we'll have to wait for that to happen."

If Mitch hadn't already been embarrassed, she would've been now. Her heart pounded and sweat formed on her forehead. "It would be good to be a major, ma'am, but it's going to take many years for that to happen. And I need to do all the right things, go to all the right places, and pass a board. It's a long way off."

"Maybe. Regardless, you'll need a whole new wardrobe. You'll need mostly dress uniforms for daytime, and civilian smart clothes for evening wear."

Mitch's eyes widened. She hadn't thought this through. She was really going to be a stuffed shirt, hovering around the ambassador at cocktail parties. She was about to stand up and say she'd changed her mind.

"I hope that I'm not making any assumptions here, but I *was* talking about pants and not actual dresses or skirts." Jessica smiled, clearly trying to allay Mitch's fears.

"There is no need to worry, ma'am, you have it right," Mitch said, taking a beat to calm herself.

'Good," Jessica said. "When can you start?"

"Officially, as soon as I've cleared it with my boss. But as far as I'm concerned, I'm with you from now on. Will I have quarters in your residence?"

"Yes, my staff will arrange that," Jessica said. "I know there's a free suite in the main house, and they'll get it ready for you."

Mitch hesitated, but since Alex was her whole reason for taking this position, she jumped in. "I'm going to ask Alex to help me with what I need, and she's likely to be a frequent visitor. I hope that's not a problem."

Jessica smiled. "I expected that, and it'll be fine. The commissioner thought you were together. Was she right? Tell me if I'm crossing a line, but I like to know my staff, and since you and I will be working together closely, I want to understand the parameters."

Mitch's stomach turned a little. She hadn't ever had a relationship where they could be considered together, let alone one that was taken into consideration in her position. "I wouldn't normally discuss my personal life, ma'am, but yes, we're together. It's new, but I'll probably spend my off-duty days with her."

"I suspect she'll be your go-to about events we'll be attending, so that's good. That can only help us. Between us all, we'll figure it out. I'll arrange your promotion and any reports that need to accompany it. Let me know if you need anything."

"Thank you, Jessica." After a few more housekeeping issues were addressed, Mitch left, and the world seemed a little sideways. She'd come to London for a conference, and she was going back to London with a new job, a new promotion, and a new woman who made her feel like she could crush rocks with her bare hands. It wasn't much more than a moment in time, and yet, her whole world had changed.

CHAPTER TWENTY-TWO

IT'D BEEN TWO WEEKS since Mitch had returned to the UK with Alex and Jessica. They'd parted with Alex at the airport, and Mitch had spent a couple of days getting herself and Jessica settled. She'd texted and spoken to Alex every day and missed her like crazy. She'd been called in to Jessica on the first day they were back and found her talking to the president, who was obviously an old friend, and she asked to speak to Mitch.

"Good morning, Madam President," Mitch said.

"Good morning, lieutenant. I understand from the ambassador that you did an excellent job with Department 6 and personally looked after her during the rescue. I'd like to thank you. It isn't often I get the chance to thank someone for going above and beyond," she said. "I've authorized your promotion to captain, and I want you to continue looking out for Jessica."

Mitch had never had anything to do with a president, but it felt pretty damn amazing. "Yes, Madam President, I'm more than happy to do that. Keeping her safe is my number one priority. And thank you for my promotion."

"If you have any problems, feel free to contact my office. I'll want to know," she said. "Now hand me back to the ambassador."

Mitch left the room and returned to her suite, where she rang her momma.

"Hey, kid. Welcome back. You are back, aren't you?"

"I just spoke to the president," Mitch said.

"The president of what?"

"The fucking President of the fucking United States, that's who." Mitch was so full of adrenaline, she couldn't stand still.

"OMG. I'll even excuse your language for that. What did she say?"

"She wanted to thank me for the operation and asked me to look after the ambassador. She's authorized my promotion too. I'm going to be a captain!" Mitch's words rolled together, and she couldn't get them out quickly enough.

"Oh, honey, I'm so proud of you."

"Could you have believed that could happen when you rescued me? You gave me so much faith in myself. I'm still learning, but Alex is keeping me in line."

"How is Alex?"

"I haven't seen her since I got back. We're meeting up later today. She's helping me with my wardrobe for all the different events, so we're going shopping. I can't say I'm looking forward to it," Mitch said.

"I'll enjoy seeing this new wardrobe of yours. Send me photos or get Alex to. I want to see how she dresses you, and how she manages it before you get fed up and leave the shop."

Mitch laughed. "I'll try to be good."

"I won't recognize you. You'll be schmoozing with the likes of the president and wearing fancy clothes," Momma said, the smile obvious in her voice.

"Can you take some vacation time and come over to meet Alex and see the sights?" Mitch asked. Her momma was one in a million, and she wanted to share her with Alex.

"Maybe, honey. I'll check and get back to you," Momma said. "I've got to shoot now. Talk soon. Love you."

"Love you, Momma." She hung up and smiled. Without her momma's patience, perseverance, and love, Mitch wouldn't even be alive, let alone in another country.

An hour later, she met up with Alex outside Department 6. "I can't keep it to myself. I talked to the president herself a while ago. It was fantastic. She thinks we did a great job. I know I'm over-excited and tripping over words, but she's backed me as a captain and asked me to take care of the ambassador. How amazing is that?"

"Wonderful." Alex wrapped her arms around Mitch and kissed her gently.

Mitch sank into the embrace and the adrenaline of the president's call slowly drained away as she calmed.

"Have you got time in your busy day of talking to presidents and ambassadors to go shopping for a new wardrobe?" Alex asked.

"I don't have a choice. And I should tell you that I hate shopping."

Alex took her hand and pulled her forward. "It's not far from here. Come on."

Within a few minutes, they were in a side street outside a small shop with suits and materials in the window, suits worn by women and men. The sign above the window read *Marsh & Jolly Ltd. LGBTQA+ specialists.*

Mitch turned to Alex. "Is this what I think it is? A shop that specializes in women like us who want suits? I didn't know they existed."

"Yes, and it's not too expensive. We can get everything you need here." Alex opened the door. "Once they have your measurements, you can always get more made just by ringing them or talking to them online." She smiled and raised her eyebrows. "No big shopping trips necessary."

Mitch pulled her in for a hard kiss. "You just keep getting better. I'm probably not going to be able to let you go, you know."

Alex bit her lip. "That's not such a bad thing."

Mitch entered after Alex, and a young man greeted them. "Good morning. Mitch? We've been expecting you."

"Pleased to meet you." Mitch smiled at his very British politeness.

"Come on through. Shelly is ready for you." He led them through the back of the shop and into a brightly lit area that had the look of a modern warehouse. "Our workshops are in the back but this area is used for measurements and suit design. It's not fancy, but it's functional."

"Hello, I'm Shelly Marsh," she said. "Thank you, Raymond. I'll take it from here. I understand that you need a new wardrobe for cocktail parties, events, and general day-to-day duties with an ambassador."

"Yeah, you got it. I want to look good. I don't want to look out of place or cheap." She'd already been thinking about having nothing good enough, and everyone knowing she came from the back hills of West Virginia.

"We can certainly fix that," Shelley said. "Let's look at what I think you might need, and you can adjust it so it feels right."

It was a smooth process, as much as it could be. Mitch liked Alex giving her input, and they managed to laugh a lot as Mitch groaned her way through standing still for measurements and choosing types of material.

"Your place or mine?" Mitch asked when the ordeal was finally over.

"Do you have time off?" Alex asked, threading her fingers through Mitch's.

"Yup, 'til 0900 hours. I need a shower, some pizza, and you. I hate to say this, but in that order," she said and grinned.

Alex laughed. "Let's see what happens when we get into the flat. Want to bet we end up having pizza heated up in the middle of the night?" She slid her hand into Mitch's back pocket and squeezed.

"Maybe...I *have* had to wait days." Mitch wrapped her arm around Alex's waist, and they headed to Alex's flat.

* * *

It was even more boring than Mitch had imagined. Jessica met with various acquaintances, and Mitch stood in the background, watching for trouble. She was introduced to some interesting people on occasion. She met Andy Green, the Chairman of Water Aid, the charity helping projects provide water, toilets, and education around the world but mostly in Africa. He was interested that she'd been in Minabo with the ambassador and told her they were raising more money to help the villages in the savannah.

"I've been in touch with the photojournalist Toni James to talk about doing a piece on the plight of the villagers who kidnapped me. She lives in London and is between assignments at the moment. Her wife is some kind of staff officer in the British Army," Jessica said.

"I've heard of her," Mitch said. "Didn't she win a big prize or something?"

"Yes, one of the highest: the Pulitzer. Anyway, she wants to take this on and will be coming to the residence while we're still on holiday."

"If and when she releases anything, I'd like to double security around you. We have no idea what the fallout might be." Mitch found she liked the element of planning and anticipation involved in this type of security. It made her think in ways she never had before.

"And that's why I've got you behind me." Jessica smiled and went back to her paperwork.

Mitch nodded, keeping her guard up, counting minutes and measuring distance. It was all new info that she wanted ingrained, should anything go sideways.

Three days and three events later, Mitch waited in the foyer for Jessica to come downstairs. She wasn't late, but Mitch liked to be five minutes early. She was dressed in her new evening suit, with vest and bow tie. She loved these new clothes and could now see why people wanted them.

Jessica came down the stairs, looking beautiful. Mitch didn't have a clue about the clothes, but Jessica had taken to testing her on the designer.

"Who am I wearing tonight, Mitch?"

"I have no idea, ma'am. Ralph Lauren?"

"You've seen me wearing two Ralph Laurens already. I'll give you a clue: the designer is spicy."

Mitch had no idea, so she shrugged.

"I knew you wouldn't get it. Victoria Beckham. She was originally one of the Spice Girls. I rather liked this dress so went for it, even though it might be a bit young for me." Jessica gave her a sweet smile.

"You look great." Mitch headed toward the door in front of Jessica, already looking out as usual. It was all clear, and then something moved in the periphery of her vision. She didn't wait to catch sight of whatever it was again. She'd seen that type of thing enough times to know. "Down!" As she pushed Jessica to the floor, she kneeled and pressed her security alarm. "Intruder alert front door. Crawl behind that armchair, ma'am, and don't come out until I tell you to."

Mitch stood and ran across the foyer, trying to keep under cover. She managed to find the light switch and turn out the lights and then crouch-ran back to the ambassador.

"I'm glad you did that," Earl said, coming out of the ambassador's study. "How can I help?"

"Ma'am, your assistant is here. Please head to the safe room with the other guards."

"We're on our way," Jessica said. "Don't take too many risks, Mitch."

"No, ma'am," she said and was on the move after they'd gone through the door leading to the safe room. "Lights out in foyer and front of building," she said quietly over the radio. "Banker safe." Banker was the secret service name for the ambassador.

"Teams moving toward the front from farther out in the grounds," the security hub said. "One team from the back of the house."

"Heading out to the front to liaise with Kite. Inform the team," Mitch said, referring to Tommy the driver.

She had to risk going outside to see what was happening. The limousine was at the bottom of the six steps outside the front door, and if she could get there, she'd have cover. She ran, taking the steps almost in one leap. There was no gunfire, which Mitch thought unusual. Either the intruders weren't in place yet, or Mitch had managed to avoid them seeing her in the dark.

Was I wrong? No She knew the way light glinted off the barrel of a rifle. She slowly opened the passenger front door of the limo and came face to face with the driver on the floor. He let out a sigh of relief when he saw it was her. "Hey, Tommy, are you hurt? Did you see anyone?"

"No, not hurt. There were two figures what ran behind the big trees at the left-hand edge of the lawn. I just caught something movin' as I turned around to get out of the car. I ducked back onto the floor."

"Stay where you are," Mitch said.

She looked over the hood of the car and then headed out into the darkening evening. She pulled her evening jacket across her chest to cover the white of her shirt and moved around the car onto the landscaped gardens. She slipped silently between the various shrubs and trees, staying in the shadows. She heard nothing. Over the radio, the team confirmed they were headed toward her position. Hopefully, they'd trap the intruders between them.

She became aware of movement ahead of her and stopped. She crouched under a sweet-smelling shrub and could make out a person in black with a rifle in the half-light. She could hear their breathing, loud and staccato. She stayed still, and the person crept slowly past her. There was a second person following, also with a rifle, but there didn't appear to be anyone else.

Mitch couldn't use her radio; she was too close. But she could try and take out the second one, though that would mean it was likely to put her into the sights of the first guy. She darted behind the second person. He wasn't much taller than her, which allowed Mitch to grab his rifle arm with one hand and grab his head to pull him back. She punched his windpipe and pushed him to the ground, keeping her hand around his throat and her knee on his sternum to choke him. His rifle fell from his grasp, and she threw it behind her into the trees. He didn't move again.

The first man turned, the whites of his eyes visible in the dark. He moved like a panther, smooth and confident, and it was obvious he was no amateur. She had to disarm him before he had a chance to take a shot. His first move was the one she'd expected. He whipped the rifle around to strike her, but she'd already ducked and moved to the side. She grabbed him around both legs and pushed herself forward from her crouched position, knocking him to the ground. She tore the rifle from his hands as he was still falling and threw it as far as she could.

She stood quickly and backed away from the man, who was on his feet as swiftly as she was. She hit him in the gut, then followed with a hook that snapped his head to the side. He reached toward his ankle, and she delivered an uppercut to his chin. He hit the ground. He tried to get to his leg again, where Mitch guessed he had a knife.

She jumped and landed on the leg he was reaching for. He screamed as something audibly snapped. But then Mitch's face exploded in a sea of pain. A second strike smashed into her nose. She managed to get another punch in before two people grabbed him, and the fight was over.

"There's another one behind me a few yards. And his rifle is somewhere close," Mitch said, blood trickling down her face.

"Yes, ma'am," one of the guards said. "We found him first, and the rest of us came around to help you out. If you come with me, we'll get you seen to by the medics."

"Is Banker safe?" Mitch asked.

"Yes, ma'am, everyone is safe. No injuries, except yourself. You'll have at least one shiner tomorrow."

Mitch headed to the front of the house, where a paramedic confirmed she had a broken nose. It wasn't out of shape, but she was told to keep an eye on it and to report to the hospital if the swelling didn't go down. She headed inside to make her report to the ambassador when her phone rang. When she saw it was Alex, she smiled but then grimaced from the pain in her face.

"How's your evening going? I half expected that you'd still be at the event, and I was going to leave you a message. Flick and Zamira are coming over to the UK, and I'd like you to meet them. Got any free time at the weekend, or early next week?"

"I'll have to get back to you, but I'd love to meet them." Mitch dabbed at the cut on her temple and winced at the pain in her nose. "As for dinner, we didn't quite get there."

"Was the ambassador ill?"

"We had an incident as we were leaving the residence. No one seriously hurt, and it's over now," Mitch said. "But I'm going to be tied up while we figure out who they are and what's going on."

"What happened? Are you okay? Is the ambassador okay? I haven't seen anything in the press or the news. Please tell me you're all right."

Mitch managed to chuckle at the barrage of questions, even through the pain. "It's only just happened. I'm okay. I promise."

"I'll come over," Alex said.

Mitch was unsure how long things would take to sort out, but she wanted to see Alex. She needed her. *That's new.*

"Is that a problem?" Alex asked.

"No," Mitch said. "I want to see you. I just don't know how long I might be with my debrief. But you being here will be good. Could you come in about an hour and wait in my suite? And bring food? I didn't get any dinner, obviously."

"See you soon," Alex said.

Mitch had never had someone that was so closely involved with her and her day-to-day life, and she liked it. It'd been something she'd never understood when other people talked about their lives with their significant others, and the togetherness in running their lives so that they overlapped. She understood it now and didn't ever want to live without it again.

CHAPTER TWENTY-THREE

ALEX DROPPED ON THE sofa at one end of the large room and pulled out her latest read. She'd always been interested in the Second World War, and *Encrypted Hearts* was proving to be a good read. Try as she might, though, she couldn't concentrate. Until she knew Mitch was really okay, she'd be unable to settle.

Alex looked up when Mitch came in, and her heart nearly stopped. Mitch's handsome face was freshly bruised and bloody. "Oh, God. What happened to you?" She almost ran across the room to take Mitch into her arms. She gave Mitch a gentle kiss on the lips and looked closely at her face. "What did the medics say?"

"Well, my nose is broken, but it'll heal. The rest of my face will be bruised, but it's nothing serious," Mitch said. "It just makes me look tough, that's all."

"I expect you'll have bruises on your knuckles as well," Alex said, lifting Mitch's hand to inspect it. She kissed the bruised areas gently.

"That makes it better," Mitch said. "But I'm not so sore I can't eat. I know you have food here somewhere; I can smell it."

"I brought beer too," Alex said.

They unpacked the meals and sat on the sofa. Alex didn't miss the way Mitch winced as she ate, and how her hands didn't seem to move very well.

"Thanks for this," Mitch said. "I might have just collapsed without eating and then woken up hangry. And I really wanted to see you."

"Did you want to talk through things with me?" Alex asked. Now that they weren't coworkers and Alex wasn't in charge, she wasn't sure where the boundaries were.

Mitch looked thoughtful. "You ground me. I was worried that what happened might stir up my nightmares again. I haven't had many since we've been together. But it'll be good to have you in my arms tonight."

"Do you think the intruders were anything to do with Minabo?" Alex asked.

"Yes, I'm certain of it. I think at least one of them was from their government," Mitch said. "They've been taken for questioning."

Alex shook her head. "I bet the ambassador was terrified."

"But now we know that extra security is still a necessity," Mitch said. "I'm going to be here for a while."

"I don't want to think about you leaving yet, but I suspect that when the time comes, things will move quickly, so we'll need to be prepared." Alex's heart pounded, and her fear took over. She already didn't want to lose Mitch, and they'd hardly started being together. There was so much more they should have, like vacations and days out. She wanted to show Mitch other places in England and take her to visit her family. But nothing in their lives would ever be predicable. "I can't think about it all today. Tell me what happened."

Mitch recounted the events of earlier in the evening, obviously trying to downplay her role in the whole takedown. Her tone was neutral, but Alex knew how these things played out. "I'm taking your memory of events with a pinch of salt, because there's no way you got those injuries with the fight you just described."

Mitch shrugged and gave her a quick smile. "At least no one was hurt or killed. That's the thing to take away, right?"

"What happens now?" Alex said. This could affect Mitch's position if the political and security experts decided that they needed a full team on the ambassador. They might even decide to send her back to the US for a while, if not permanently.

"I'm going to take a shower and then let you kiss my wounds and make them all better," Mitch said.

Alex let the serious matters go. There'd be time for them later.

"Can I join you? It'll help with my medical assessment of where best to concentrate my healing efforts."

"Sounds like valid logic," Mitch said. "I'll get it running."

Alex cleared away the mess from the meal and stripped her clothes off. She went into the bathroom and watched Mitch in the shower, her heart racing as she stared. She was already thinking of what she wanted to do to Mitch.

"Stop looking and get in here," Mitch said. "I want to soap you from top to bottom, and in all those little places that I've grown to love."

Alex got into the shower, and Mitch pulled her into a hug to get her under the water before she started to soap her. She didn't hurry, and the feel of Mitch's hands massaging her breasts took Alex's breath away. "Don't play too much, I desperately want you, and I don't want teasing tonight."

Mitch put her hand between Alex's legs and slipped her fingers through the wetness. She pulled Alex's leg up to her waist, and the water from the showerhead cascaded gently between them.

"The thought that you were injured has made me need to feel you," Alex said. "I need you inside me. Prove to me you're okay."

Mitch entered her, and Alex moaned. "More... More and harder."

Mitch filled her, and the rhythm of her movements was just what Alex needed. She looked into Mitch's eyes as she came, and her leg on the shower floor gave way under her. Mitch held her up. "Don't move that hand," Alex said.

"I can't," Mitch said and laughed. "Your grip won't let me go."

"I don't want to." Sometimes soft and gentle was good, but at times like this, Alex just needed Mitch to take her hard. She pushed Mitch against the shower wall and went down on her knees, wasting no time in putting her fingers between her wet folds. Mitch's clit was swollen, and she was obviously ready for release. Alex followed her fingers with her mouth, and loved Mitch's taste, which reminded her of warm summer days.

"I'm ready to explode," Mitch said, her eyes closed, and her head back against the tile.

Alex pushed two fingers inside her and used her tongue to tease Mitch's clit. Mitch held her shoulders.

"Yes, Alex," she said. "Yes."

Mitch shuddered, and Alex removed her fingers. Mitch slid onto her knees and rested her head on Alex's shoulder, and they remained that way until the water began to cool.

"I'll get us towels," Alex said and kissed Mitch's nose gently, before getting up on unsteady legs. She opened a bath towel and wrapped it around Mitch as she came out of the shower, then she found another towel for herself. She dried Mitch carefully around her many bruises. "I expect these are all starting to hurt. I've got a couple of ibuprofen you should take; it'll help with the pain."

"Fighting two intruders and having sex might've worn me out," Mitch said and smiled.

Alex swallowed hard. How could she feel as much as she did after such little time? There was no doubt she was falling in love with Mitch. She just hoped that they could weather the storm of trying to stay together when their work tried to pull them apart. But what if Mitch didn't feel the same?

She shook her head to get rid of the thoughts and soon they tumbled into bed, both exhausted. Alex expected to fall asleep quickly after the day she'd had, but she was wide awake. Thoughts of an uncertain future nagged at her. Department 6 was happy with her and the way she'd handled the mission, and there was no question she'd be given more in the future. Things were good, but what about her and Mitch? Really, she had no choice but to accept things as they were and let them be what they would. But that was easier said than done. She drifted to sleep, comforted by the weight of Mitch's hand resting on her hip.

Morning sunlight filtered into the room, and she woke slowly. When she opened her eyes, she found Mitch already watching her.

"Hello, beautiful," Mitch said. "Why do I feel like I slammed into a concrete pillar yesterday?"

"It looks like you did too. I guess you must have," Alex said.

"I also realized something yesterday, something important," Mitch said. "I have something I need to say."

Alex's heart sank. It sounded like one of *those* conversations was about to happen.

"I need you," Mitch said. "I wanted you last night, but not just for sex or some kind of outlet. Because you make me feel safe, like someone actually cares about me. It's something I never thought I'd say, but if that's what love is, then I love you." Vulnerability shone in her eyes. "I love you, and you need to know I'm in it for the long run...if you want me."

She loves me. Alex had sworn off a relationship with anyone who did a similar job, and yet here she was, in love with someone who made her heart flutter and her world more vibrant than she could ever have imagined it would be. "I think I loved you from almost the beginning. You drive me mad, and loving you is going to be an adventure." She kissed her softly, gently cupping her cheek. "No matter what happens, we'll find a way to make this work."

Mitch's smile could have rivaled the light of the sun, and she rolled on top of Alex. "Say it again."

"I love you." She punctuated it with another kiss, this one full of fire. "Now show me how much you love me."

Mitch did exactly that, over and over again. When Mitch got a text asking her to come to a debrief in the afternoon, and to bring Alex with her, she was happy she wouldn't need to leave Mitch's side. It was too perfect, too fresh, to leave behind today. They were each other's safe place, and whatever came, they'd face it side by side.

EPILOGUE

IT SEEMED LIKE IT was only yesterday that Alex had friends at her house in Norfolk, but it was actually over six months ago, before meeting Mitch, and before Minabo. Since Africa, she and Mitch had come up to Norfolk whenever they could to get away from their work to decompress. Though there hadn't been any more intruders, the feeling of tension and potential violence remained. Mitch was still the ambassador's bodyguard and had settled into life in the residence and would even say that she enjoyed the job. She'd certainly taken to wearing the gorgeous suits, of which she now had a closet full.

After dinner, they sat lazily around the lounge with glasses of whiskey.

"So what are you up to at work, Flick?" Mitch asked. "Alex doesn't give me nearly enough gossip."

Flick grinned. "I've been asked to help Neela get into the swing of operations in Department 6. We're going to do a couple of low-risk retrievals around France and Italy, but once she's up and running, I think she'll be one of our star operators."

"Is it good to be back home, Neela?" Alex asked. She'd been excited to get the call from her, letting her know she was coming back.

"It is. I can't tell you how much I appreciate you renting me your flat," Neela said.

"Well, you saved me having to advertise it," Alex said. "It's just not big enough for two of us. And although Mitch has her room in the embassy, we need somewhere to spread out if we stay in town for a day or two. Her room doesn't cut it."

"I'm all settled in, but I'll be spending most of the next few months in France. I'm going to stay with Flick and Zamira while Flick puts me through my training."

"What's happening with the ambassador, Mitch?" Flick asked.

"Toni James ran with the story," Mitch said. "Between her own sources and the ambassador's, they managed to get all sorts of information that proved the aid money was lining the pockets of government officials, as well as some of the senior army staff. Although the US probably won't get that aid money back. And they think there are still some criminals who haven't been uncovered, but at least that channel has been reopened. Aid workers have been sent to the area to get things moving, and they're meeting with tribal elders to make it happen."

"The ambassador has been much more political, and Mitch thinks she'll probably stay another year to deal with the projects she's got on," Alex said.

"That means we have another year to work out what we're going to do with our lives when this phase finishes. Neither of our governments are happy that we're together, the UK more so than the US, because the UK is worried that I'm stealing all your Department 6 secrets from Alex." Mitch grinned and gave Alex a wink.

"What are you thinking of doing about it?" Flick asked.

Alex and Mitch shared a smile. They'd been doing a lot of talking and planning, but all they really needed and wanted was each other.

"Alex is going to take a leave of absence from Department 6, and I'll retire." Mitch laughed at the comments that she wasn't old enough to do so. "I've done my twenty years, and I'm tired of getting shot at. Maybe the only adrenaline rush I need is from being with Alex." She laughed again at the gagging noises and groans that came her way. "Anyway. We're thinking of heading to some countries we've never been to so we can enjoy ourselves without living in the shadows."

"It's the best idea we've had so far," Alex said. "It means we can carry on our journey together and see where it takes us." As long as it took them somewhere together, anywhere they went would be perfect. And maybe the traveling wouldn't last forever; she wasn't convinced that either of them could give up their missions. But whatever the future held for them, Alex *was* convinced she could face anything with Mitch at her side.

~ THE END ~

I really hope you enjoyed reading *Love Under Fire*. If you did, it would be wonderful if you could pop a little review on Amazon.

Like the thought of all these amazing, strong women running all over the world on important missions? Then you might like to read *Breakout for Love*, the first in the Dept. 6 series. You'll also find out how Flick and Zamira got together!

And if you want to keep up to date with my writer life, along with all my lovely author colleagues over at Butterworth Books, you might like to sign up for their monthly newsletter (b t.ly/ButterBookers).

Thank you,
Valden

Other Great Butterworth Books

Breakout for Love by Valden Bush
They're both running from their pasts. Together, they might make a new future.
Available from Amazon (ASIN B0CWHZ4SXL)

Death in Time by RJ Nyx
Book 3 in The Extractor trilogy: Working in the past is hell on your future.
Available on Amazon (ASIN B0DWG24C66)

Here in My Heart by Jo Fletcher
In the golden glow of a South of France autumn, two very different lives collide.
Available on Amazon (ASIN B0FCHNLK9W)

Sapphic Eclectic Volumes 1 to 6 edited by Nyx & Willows
A little something for everyone...
Available free from the Butterworth Books website

The Heart Remembers by Ally McGuire
One wedding. One ex. And one week of chaos that might just lead to forever.
Available on Amazon (ASIN B0F932F8LZ)

The Sister Act by Helena Harte
She's faking it for one sister, but will she end up falling for the other?
Available from Amazon (ASIN B0F4KSVCZ9)

Change in Time by RJ Nyx
Book 2 in The Extractor trilogy: Working in the past is hell on your future.
Available on Amazon (ASIN B0DWG24C66)

Racing Hearts by Sydney Lear
Life in the fast lane is great...until you lose control.
Available from Amazon (ASIN B0DZP9X3G2)

Driving Me Barking by JP Preston
Sometimes the one who got away never really left..
Available on Amazon (ASIN B0DWG1LLXN)

Escape in Time by RJ Nyx
Book 1 in The Extractor trilogy: Working in the past is hell on your future.
Available on Amazon (ASIN B0DSJFDZ7R)

Ship of Dreams by Brey Willows
Two rival captains, one deadly mission. Secrets that will set the skies ablaze.
Available on Amazon (ASIN B0DRW1X75N)

Unwritten by Helena Harte
No strings is fun 'til it unravels.
Available from Amazon (ASIN B0DGQFFHYB)

Chucking Putty at the Queen by Simon Smalley
A heartbreaking, humorous, and courageous exploration of self-discovery.
Available from Amazon (ASIN B0DGGBV22W)

The Promise by Addison M Conley
When the world keeps pulling you under, who do you reach for?
Available on Amazon (ASIN B0DDY9FH6Z)

Back to Back by Jo Fletcher
.When Fred and Ruby's worlds collide, can love rise from the rubble?
Available on Amazon (ASIN B0D6M499K2)

Heart of the Storm by Ally McGuire
Sometimes a storm is just what you need to clear the skies ahead.
Available on Amazon (ASIN B0CYTSQXWW)

Sanctuary by Helena Harte
Passions ignite and possibilities unfold. Welcome to the Windy City Romance series.
Available from Amazon (ASIN B0D4B42RRW)

Brave Enough to Love by Valden Bush
In a dance between truth and sacrifice, can they rewrite the rules of love?
Available on Amazon (ASIN B0CQP8PMVB)

Dead Ringer by Robyn Nyx
Three bodies. One killer. No motive?
Available on Amazon (ASIN B0CPQ8HFK7)

Medea by JJ Taylor
Who will Medea become in her battle for freedom?
Available from Amazon (ASIN B0CK2FB7GW)

Scripted Love by Helena Harte
What good is a romance writer who doesn't believe in happy ever after?
Available on Amazon (ASIN B0993QFLNN)

Call to Me by Helena Harte
Sometimes the call you least expect is the one you need the most.
Available on Amazon (ASIN B08D9SR15H)

What's Your Story?

Global Wordsmiths, CIC, provides an all-encompassing service for all writers, ranging from basic proofreading and cover design to development editing, typesetting, and eBook services. A major part of our work is charity and community focused, delivering writing projects to under-served and under-represented groups across Nottinghamshire, giving voice to the voiceless and visibility to the unseen.

To learn more about what we offer, visit: www.globalwords.co.uk

A selection of books by Global Words Press:
Desire, Love, Identity: with the National Justice Museum
Aventuras en México: Farmilo Primary School
Times Past: with The Workhouse, National Trust
Young at Heart with AGE UK
In Different Shoes: Stories of Trans Lives